# THE TEXTBOOK OF THE ROSE

## A TALE

### JOANN MCCAIG

CORMORANT
BOOKS

The publisher gratefully acknowledges the support of the
Canada Council for the Arts and the Ontario Arts Council for
its publishing program. We acknowledge the financial support
of the Government of Canada through the Book
Publishing Industry Development Program (BPIDP)
for our publishing activities.

THE CANADA COUNCIL | LE CONSEIL DES ARTS
FOR THE ARTS | DU CANADA
SINCE 1957 | DEPUIS 1957

Printed and bound in Canada.

Canadian Cataloguing in Publication Data

McCaig, JoAnn, 1953-
The textbook of the rose

ISBN 1-896951-23-6

I. Title.
PS8575.C345T49 2000   C813'.54   C99-901526-5
PR9199.3.M33T49 2000

CORMORANT BOOKS INC.
RR 1, Dunvegan, Ontario  K0C 1J0

*for my sons*

*passus*: [Lat.] literally 'a step': a section of a poem, i.e. a stage in its development. A section, division, or canto of a story or poem.

*chanson d'aventure*: [Fr.] a type of poem developed in France in the twelfth century which treats of unexpected love-meetings, usually in a pastoral setting.

# PROLOGUE

June 1997

FRIDAY NIGHT

Spiderman. Gotta love the guy. Not that I've ever watched a single episode, but I've heard them all, as I stand in the kitchen wiping placemats and scraping carrots while the kids sprawl semi-comatose on the family-room couch. So there he is in the thick of the battle between good and evil, his rival Venom retching and puking in the background — Why do all the villains have serious vocal disorders? Venom, Darth Vader ... why can't they sound mellifluous, silky, like real-life bad guys? — anyway, world domination is at stake once again, but there's Spidey, ducking into a smouldering building to take a breather and ask the big question: "I wonder if being a superhero keeps me apart from the ones I love?"

And I contemplate the heartache of a superhero's life with him, scraping orange goop off the sides of a saucepan, till I hear the sound of Jake's truck idling in the driveway. "Dad's here, TV off please, have you got all your stuff?" Zak and Miranda scurry and flurry, and Jake shouts from the back door, "Stella, where's his ball glove?"

Had I known there was a woman in the passenger seat, I wouldn't have come outside. My mouth is still numb from two hours of root planing in the dentist's chair, coffee splattered down the front of my shirt, and I have to lift my upper lip manually to form a smile. This month's selection is young, looks Asian. She and I give each other the finger wave, four fingers rise and fall in succession, toodle-oo, and I know that before the truck has cleared the end of the drive, I will have taken to my bed. I still get blindsided sometimes ... but he doesn't bring them around, hardly ever any more, not like before. Especially not like that first time, three years ago, the first time I took to my bed, *her* smug profile a cruel body blow.

Once, when I was twenty-one, I was hitching down-island from a summer job, and the guy who picked me up was a manager with Mac-and-Blo, coming down from meetings up north. Charlie was his name — executive haircut, pressed pants, company car. He said he was going to Victoria for the night, said he was meeting A Friend. The word *Friend* bore weight; it meant that the person he was meeting was not a man. The guy was married; it was my policy to check for a wedding ring the minute I got into the car. Not that it made much difference most of the time. But Charlie — God, he was smooth. I was just glad of the ride and the clean car and the fact that he was sober. Cresting the Malahat, Charlie says, "I'm staying at the Empress. My Friend and I. Where are you staying tonight?"

"With friends," I said. No capital letter, just a crash pad in Fernwood. I'd be lucky to find a couch cushion to curl up on, much less a bed. A bunch of us were heading over to Vancouver the next day. The Dead were playing the Coliseum Saturday night. I would meet Jake there, for the first time, but I didn't know that yet.

Charlie said, "Why don't you come downtown and have a drink with me? My Friend's plane doesn't get in till six."

The tavern at the Empress was a dank little hole called The Beaver. Charlie said no, he'd rather go to The Library, a lounge bar off the main lobby. But the barman stopped us at the door and looked me up and down. I'd been working at the Forestry nursery near Comox, bent over rows of seedlings, pulling up weeds. I'd showered at camp, but my clothes could've used a wash. "Sorry, sir, but we can't let the young lady in. No jeans allowed."

"Well, I guess we'll just have to have a drink upstairs, then," Charlie said, grinning.

His room was on the third floor. Tall windows draped with ornate sheers and valances, overlooking the harbour. A massive bed with a thick coverlet in satiny peach and grey. Charlie pulled a bottle out of his suitcase, brought two glasses from the bathroom, said, "I'll grab some ice." I didn't move or look around. I was watching the harbour. I was waiting to see what would happen. The door closed, then opened again. "By the way, Stella, if the phone rings——"

"Yeah?"

"Don't pick it up, okay?" He said this cheerfully.

We stood at the window, drinking Scotch, watching throngs of tourists disgorge from double-decker buses painted with the Union Jack, watching harried mothers push infants in collapsible strollers. And after a time, a seaplane appeared out of nowhere, then touched down like a bright bauble on the glittering water. The AirBC commuter from Vancouver.

"We better get down there," Charlie said.

"We," that's what he said.

I drained my glass and set it down on the table beside his, hoisted my knapsack, and followed him down the corridor, into the elevator, through the lobby, and out the front doors. Was it curiosity, obedience, inertia? Or mere heartlessness? I don't know. I just went along, pushing through the heavy brass doors at the front of the hotel, skirting impossibly tidy flower beds, waiting at the crosswalk as we watched the seaplane manoeuvre into its berth at the pier.

We crossed the street as the ladder came down and the passengers emerged, among them a tall brunette who carefully adjusted her hair and sunglasses before raising her head to look

around. Charlie called out, "Michelle!" She turned, smiled —
then she noticed me and her smile cracked, and took a full beat
to recompose itself. Charlie said, "Hi, you made it. Great. I'd
like you to meet Stella."

Michelle wore pressed linen slacks — off white — a tailored jacket, a crisp shirt with muted pinstripes. The beige sling-
backs were a mistake, but you could see she'd dressed with exquisite care. No wedding ring. Even her overnight bag was new,
probably bought expressly for this occasion. Charlie lifted his
arm to my shoulder in a gesture that was slightly less than a hug
and said, "Well, I guess we better get settled. You take care now,
Stella. Have fun at that concert." My bit part was over — a
serendipitous entrance, an exit on cue. I hoisted my pack and
said, "Nice to meet you, Michelle. Take it easy, Charlie."

Next day, lined up outside the Coliseum with a hangover
that just wouldn't quit, at least until somebody handed me a
quarter of windowpane, I kept thinking about Charlie and
Michelle. In a few hours, Jake would waltz up to me and whirl
me like a dervish all the way through "Saint Stephen." But then,
I just kept thinking about Charlie and Michelle, imagining their
languorous hours on that peach and grey coverlet, with the
sounds of the harbour outside the big windows. I kept replaying the scene where Michelle alights from that heavenly white
plane in her linen pants — this adult scenario — expensive and
serious. So removed from the world I knew — sweat and draft
beer and regular visits to the Free Clinic.

Charlie never made a single move on me. He didn't need
to. He had other uses for me.

I forgive him that. I even forgive him the credit-card slips I
know he left lying around for his wife. But that look — that
crumbling smile on Michelle's face — unforgivable. Sheer terror. The chasm opening right under her feet ... I bet Charlie
still gets hard every time he remembers it. I bet that night by
the harbour was the best sex he ever had in his life.

Friday night. Diana finally returns my call, half an hour after Jake and the kids leave. I'm furious, "Why the hell didn't you tell me you weren't going to apply? They posted the sessionals this afternoon——"

"Because I knew you'd try to talk me out of it. Actually, I did apply and then withdrew at the end of May. Look, Stella, I've got to get Adam to soccer, I'll see you Sunday. The usual. All right?"

As Zak would say, *Wanna know what really sucks?* The reign of terror grinds on.

The day my son was born, I died, briefly. I was in what the manuals call "transition" — mine was the most thoroughly re-searched first pregnancy in history, not that it did me any good — when I suddenly could not locate my own body in space. The doctor and midwife were barking orders, telling me to calm down, not understanding that I no longer knew where my legs and arms were. I heard a panicky edge in the doctor's voice — "anesthesiology STAT, episiotomy tray STAT" — and then noth-ing.

Till Jake's voice, from across the universe. "Stel, listen. Can you hear something?" A small cry. I couldn't see or talk or move, but I could hear. They lay the baby on the pillow beside my head, and placed my hands on him, hands stiff with IV needles and bloodied tape. My vision returned in flashes, but weirdly, like looking through translucent glass, the kind with that bee-hive design, interlocking hexagons to infinity.

Jake said, "He's going to be fine. They had to give him some oxygen, but he's——" Then a *thwump*, spinal cord haywire, my almost-last words were — no, let Jake tell it, he tells it so well:

"So they've just taken the baby down to NICU, getting ready to move Stella into the recovery room, but she looks agitated and I can see she's trying to speak, so I lean close and she says 'Swzzhapazzaga,' and I go, 'What?' and she goes, 'I think I'm going spazzy again.' And then she starts to seize: her face just stretches like a death mask, and her back arches and falls, *whamwham*, like something out of *The Exorcist,* and I'm thinking: Holy fuck, man, this is it, we're gonna lose her. I yell for help and a dozen people race into the room, and all I could think was: 'God, please don't let those be Stella's last words, she'd be so pissed off—'"

SATURDAY NIGHT

My movie selection is *Sea of Love*. The Gretz recommended it to me a few months ago, when she was Between Men. She said, "I've been watching a lot of erotic thrillers lately, I don't know why." Gretz is never between men for very long; I wonder if she knows how much I hate her. I saw her yesterday after work. Rush hour. I've spent the morning teaching, noon hour in a typically vicious department meeting, and the afternoon in the dentist's chair. I've just dropped Miranda off at skating, and I'm picking Zak up at his counselling appointment. The freezing still hasn't come out, but I'm so faint with hunger that I'm grazing for leftovers on the floor of the car, seriously contemplating a week-old French fry, and there, at a crosswalk, is The Gretz. Downtown baby — a London Fog trench with belt tied, not fastened; the calfskin briefcase; Yves St. Laurent pantihose with Reebok crosstrainers — and she's smiling up at the man at her side. They're probably off to the Black Cat for martinis and calamari, and, afterwards, who knows? And me, I'm stuck in traffic, grazing granola-bar crumbs and bruised apple while my son talks to a stranger at eighty bucks an hour and Daddy's little angel twirls in her skating dress, her head spinning with that fairy-tale shit, and I am so goddamn furious I could grab that trenchcoat belt, wrap it around Gretz's neck, and just squeeze ...

Anyhow, *Sea of Love* opens on a man having sex with someone you can't see, his bare ass pumping, his voice muttering panicky endearments in the last few seconds of his life, before he is shot by the unknown person who has been witnessing his performance at gunpoint, finding out the identity of whom is the whole point of the story. The good thing about videos is the pause button.

The dog follows me into the bathroom, settles herself on the mat to observe the proceedings with affectionate interest. Probably she's just being polite. After all, don't I watch her in the field behind the house every day? Don't I stand there with a bread bag turned inside out over my hand, crooning encouragements? Good dog, good girl!

I contemplate the crotch of my underpants, and think of all the women in this city, in the world, who are right at this moment contemplating the crotch of *their* underpants, praying for a sign: yea or nay, reprieve or disaster, triumph or disappointed hopes. The few occasions in a woman's life when the absence of blood is welcome.

I note that Winnie the Pooh is bleeding shampoo from the hole in the top of his head and I tenderly dab it up with a wad of toilet paper. *Finis des larmes* — no more tears.

Zak and I stayed in hospital for two weeks, but, at the end of the first week, my doctor sent me home on a day pass. I was feeling like a kid who's done too many underwater somersaults and is having trouble swimming back up to the light. Every time the nurses teased me about "misbehaving in delivery," I thought they meant I'd screamed and cried too much. So the Sunday afternoon after Zak was born, I got this day pass, and Jake drove me home. I went straight to the bedside table and looked up "eclampsia" in my encyclopedia of pregnancy. I read that eclampsia is fatal to one in twenty mothers, and to one infant in five. "I need to go back, Jake. Right now."

At the corner by the Esso Station, a shape fluttering in the breeze, like a huge peony, pale pink tinged with white. No, not a peony, a group of women, four old women, gussied up for a Sunday outing, every one of them dressed in some combination of pastel pink and white. Their bus approached on the other side of the street, right in front of the dry cleaners'. The old ladies fluttered and laughed, darting cautious glances at the Walk signal and the traffic, then tottered across the street on pale veiny legs, in white summer sandals. The light changed and, though I craned my neck, I never saw whether they made it or not. At that moment I had no more fervent prayer in all the world but for their safe deliverance.

*Sea of Love* is over, violins swell — God, how I hate Hollywood endings. I undress at the bedroom mirror, liking what I see, especially the new underwear. If I stand up straight, I look damn good for forty-one. This is the gift I give myself each night, before bed. Then I turn away from the mirror to bend over, not wanting to see the dugs that hang, the corrugated bellyflesh, the loose abdomen that disengages from my pelvis like an up-turned porridge bowl. Small mercy, genial self-deception — a few more years before I undress in the dark. Around 11:30, as every night, the dog clambers out of her basket in the TV room, wanders over to her water dish and laps noisily, then patters down the hall to my room. *Ka-tippa-tippa-tippa* on the hardwood. If my light is still on, she comes to my side of the bed for a pat. If it's off, she keeps going, around to the far side, Jake's side. *Ka-tippa-tippa.* Pause. *Ka-tip,* turns. A grunt, an "oof," the scraping of claws as she settles herself on the floor, the clang of her tags against the wood. She smacks her black and pink lips a few times, then sleeps.

Some time later, as every night, come the random beeps. Something, somewhere in the house — the watch Zak's grandma sent him for Christmas, maybe? — beeps eight or nine times, then falls silent. Where do the random beeps come from? Is the watch — or whatever it is — stuffed in a drawer, underneath a couch cushion, hidden beneath a basket of toys? The random beeps, the way they catch me off guard night after night, make me wonder if some people can just be born with excess innocence, like being born with an extra finger. Or without foresight, like a missing organ. Not a vital one — say, one kidney when two would be better. Every night, the random beeps startle me awake just as I'm drifting off. I hear them and think: I've got to figure out where that comes from, then I forget all about it till the next night, when I'm nearly asleep. A few times, I've jumped out of bed, but the random beeps stop before I'm even through the bedroom door. Persons maimed by excess innocence and insufficient foresight wake up each morning surprised and dismayed to find the clock moving steadily toward the last minute possible to leave for work; to find that lunches must, yet again, be made; that spilled cereal waits to be wiped from vinyl placemats, along with globs of ketchup from last night's supper. Sometimes I feel condemned to a life of dismayed surprise.

Before they left on Friday night to spend the weekend with their father and the Bonk of the Month, I prepared dinner for my children according to the package directions, cooking it *to the desired tenderness.* Then Zak and Miranda left, and I took to my bed, pondering what *the desired tenderness* might be. I thought of how Victorian women used to take to their beds, achieve exemption. Women in my mother's day had "nervous breakdowns," or the poorer ones "cracked up." After JFK was shot, Jackie went "into seclusion." How I loved that phrase, *innntooo seh-cloooooo-zhun,* how inviting, how peaceful. No such luxury for us, these days. We receive medications, counselling, stacks of self-help books. Somebody must have noticed the value of our labour.

The first time I took to my bed was three years ago. Jake dropped the bomb one Tuesday night and ever since then, I'd been driving into the parkade each morning and hanging on to the steering wheel, muttering *Please, God, help me survive the next six hours and I'll be okay,* and then I'd drive home from work, clutching the steering wheel and praying, *Please God, just help me get through till Zak and Miranda go to bed and then I'll be okay.* And so, on the Friday night, Jake calls and says he'd like to pick up the kids and take them out for dinner. "Fine," I say. "They're pretty freaked out about all this. They need to see you." And he pulls up in front of our house with *her* sitting in the passenger seat. Did he instruct her to stare straight ahead, not to turn her head one millimetre, to present only a sedate profile? Her invention, more likely. Which of them enjoyed putting me to this use the most? Primary source, secondary source. Miranda skipped off: "Daddy!" — arms around his neck. Zak saw me at the window, saw me turn and stumble down the hall toward the bedroom. I dimly heard the front door creak, and muffled voices on the lawn, and then the door opened again.

My son sat with me all that evening. My son sat in silence on the bedroom chair while I lay there in the dark, stretched out on my bed like a figure on a tomb. I couldn't cry or talk or move. It took everything I had merely to *withstand* it.

SUNDAY NIGHT

Car doors slam outside and my children tumble into the house. Each of them carries a small red object. A little sports car, with a mechanical wind-up key on the back, and a cellophane-wrapped packet of peppermints inside. An airport gift, the kind you buy for a child you've never met.

"Hi guys, I just phoned for the pizza. It should be here any minute. How was your weekend?"

"Great," says Miranda. "See what Karen gave us?"

"Her name's Carmen, stupid. It was okay. What did you do, Mom?"

"Let's see. I did some marking, and had coffee with Diana, and had coffee with Gretz, and walked the dog, and watched a movie, and ... that's about it. What did you guys do?"

"Hung around, mostly," Zak says. "Played Nintendo. I got to the vanilla-donut level and went through that door to where the treasure is."

Miranda plunks herself in my lap, throws her thin arms around my neck, and plants a sticky kiss on my cheek. She says, "And Mom, on Saturday, we went out for dinner to the neatest place. The people are *sooo* nice. And everybody there knows Daddy. Every single waitress in the place knows what his favourite kind of beer is."

"Wow. That's great."

"Oh yeah. Daddy wants you to drive me to skating tomorrow because he's thrown his back out again and he has to go to the doctor."

"Sure, no problem. I thought Daddy was kind of hobbling when he walked you up the driveway. Too bad, huh?" I manage not to laugh. Till later, when the phone rings and a cheerful male voice says, "This is Darren from Domino's and I'm just calling to see how your pizza experience was tonight."

And I can't help it, I literally squeal with laughter and barely choke out the words, "Our pizza experience? Oh, God ... Sorry ... Darren, our pizza experience was ... the best ... fabulous."

Darren is offended. He says, icily, "Glad to hear it, ma'am. Thank you so much for your time."

After the kids have gone to bed, the little cars lie forgotten on the living-room floor. That night, I dream that I am walking down a corridor as if I were a character in a Philip Marlowe movie, black and white. I trip over the little cars. I walk up to a door with semi-translucent glass. I peer through the glass, this crazy honeycomb pattern, and see a hundred images of four old ladies running for a bus, each one in *Father Knows Best* cotton dresses with ballooning skirts, all pastel pink and white. One turns to me and says, *Neverleavechildunattended*, another pulls a Little Black Sambo doll out of her capacious string bag and tries to force it into my hand. The third has her back to me, but then she turns her grey head and she has Charlotte's face. Her red-lipsticked mouth forms the words *my hero,* but no sound comes. The last woman is scrambling up the stairs to the bus, and I am so relieved. But she pauses, she adjusts her sunglasses and her dark, shoulder-length hair before turning to look at me with such loathing that I wake up gasping. As I wander the darkened house, I can hear the dog chomping away at something in the living room. I suspect it's the souvenir candies but decide to delay confirmation, willing to await the dog's guiltily peppermint-scented farts tomorrow morning. Besides, if I pretend not to notice, maybe someone else will clean up the mess.

*PASSUS ONE*

DEFENCE
March 1994

## 1. A Dinner Party

So far, so good, Jake standing next to her at the kitchen counter, easing the cork from the bottle. "Taste," he says.

"I can't. I'm a non-drinker. But it smells nice," Charlotte says, thinking that if this isn't too much of a disaster, she might throw a big party after June convocation.

"But this is a celebration. You could just try it."

"No thanks. I quit drinking when I was expecting my daughter and never started again."

Stella joins them. "What's this? You don't drink? Well, who drank up all that champagne I bought after the defence?"

"The committee, I guess," Charlotte says, not adding, *And you.*

"How could I not have noticed?" Stella says.

"My personal cataclysms. I seem to think I have to make an offering ..." Charlotte hesitates, then risks it. "With the thesis, for example, I gave up sex."

"Took yourself to a nunnery, did you?" Jake is laughing.

"Yup, from the first word of the first draft right through the defence."

Jake and Stella are riveted. They speak at once. Charlotte has scored.

Stella: "What a cipher!"

Jake: "*When* was the defence?"

Stella: "It might have relaxed you."

Jake: "So it's been three days."

Stella: "Though admittedly, men, or lovers" — catching herself making assumptions — "can be terribly distracting."

Jake snickers. "Let's see, the defence was ... when?"

"Tuesday."

"And?" Jake's not a bad-looking man, for his age. A little scruffy, maybe.

"I have a date tomorrow night."

They are carrying their glasses into Charlotte's living room, settling themselves, a sprightly Vivaldi concerto on the disc changer, candlelight. Maya has done a lovely job on the table, except that the cutlery is backwards.

"Tell us more. Who's the lucky man?" This is a Stella that Charlotte has never seen, giggly and schoolgirlish, light of heart.

"Oh just somebody I met in a coffee shop a few months ago. Nice guy, lives out in one of those new subdivisions, divorced. He's been asking me out for a while, and I kept putting him off. But we met for a drink the night after the defence."

"And?"

"It was fine. So we have a dinner date tomorrow night." She doesn't say it's at his place. It's a fine dance, this. She wants to be interesting but not to reveal too much. With people like Jake and Stella, you have to be dead on, so right, so hard, so precise. So smart.

Jake asks: "How can you go for a drink if you don't drink?"

"I tend to consider that one of my many sterling qualities: I'm a cheap date. I just nurse a glass of ginger ale all night. I mean, Wednesday night, the guy offered to buy me dinner too, wanted to take me to The Keg or something, and I said, 'Oh no, it's such a nice warm evening, why don't we just go to a drive-through and grab a burger and find ourselves a park bench?'"

"You *are* a cheap date," Stella remarks, approvingly.

"Well, the two of you wouldn't know this, but dating in the nineties is fraught with peril, and I hate to think of being stuck in some restaurant with a guy and, poof, you run out of conversation halfway through the salad."

"Perilous," Stella concurs. "What does this nice man do for a living?"

"He's in sales. Oilfield equipment, I think. Oh hi, honey. Maya, I'd like you to meet my supervisor, Stella Morrison. And her husband, Jake. This is my daughter, Maya."

It has never failed in all these nine years: The flicker of shock, the quick intake of breath, the composure of the social face, when people meet the dark-skinned daughter of a blue-eyed mother. "Pleased to meet you," says Jake solemnly, and shakes Maya's thin brown hand.

A month after her mother died, Charlotte went to Club Med on St. Thomas. That's where she met Maya's father, a tall, laughing stringbean of a man, a cocktail wizard, the smell of grenadine and lime on his long tapered fingers. She took him to her room the night they met, and every night after. They'd wake at dawn, sneak out of the compound, past the groomed hedges of hibiscus glistening against the stucco walls studded discreetly with barbs, and she'd drive him home, to the turnoff half a mile from the pastel chattel house where he lived with his wife and children. On their last morning, just outside the hotel, Charlotte glimpsed a figure trudging down the road, a pale brown young woman, heavily made up, bleached stiff hair in wild tufts, a satiny red tube top and tight black skirt, spike heels dangling from her fingers as she picked her way barefoot along the side of the road, watching for broken glass. She looked stunned, brutally hung over. From their car, the tall black man and the small white woman gazed as they drove past, Charlotte hoping that at least the girl had a wad of bills stashed somewhere beneath her cheap skimpy clothes, while the man beside her chuckled, "Mos' likely *her* pussy hurtin' this mornin'."

The meal is a moderate success. Charlotte's fridge has been on the blink, and the salad is lightly frozen. The rice is sticky and there's not enough of it, but the curried shrimp tastes fine and the corn bread from the Portuguese bakery atones for other sins. Maya rises to the occasion — give the kid credit for sensing how much this evening counts — and, instead of whining for the TV or sliding a Green Day tape into the stereo, she makes polite conversation, asking Jake whether he's ever seen that episode of *The Simpsons* where the kids get head lice and are taken away from their parents. Jake has, as a matter of fact. Turns out that he loves *The Simpsons*, watches it every day.

Charlotte has heard rumours, but tonight Jake and Stella seem so companionable, sitting together on the couch after the meal, drinking wine. Jake tells the harrowing tale of their son's birth, and they laugh and try to recall all the Famous Last Words they know. When they run out of those, they begin to make them up. Charlotte's favourite is the one Jake made up for Shakespeare: "I said 'sullied' and I meant 'sullied,' asshole!" Charlotte adores these people, adores their company, their conversation. It seems to her a miracle to have such people at her table, in her life.

Stella is what Charlotte wants to be. Stella has held Charlotte in her hands, has created her, no — has permitted Charlotte to create herself. Invested her with authority. Does Stella know how every syllable of every conversation they've ever had is cherished, analysed, replayed? "Go to the site of your oppression" is something Stella said to her once, and Charlotte has made it her mantra. Stella plays her role masterfully, making gentle nudges and pronouncements, the personal meted out only anecdotally, to make a point. Tonight, though, Stella is Charlotte's guest. Dinner guest. Tonight Stella and Charlotte stand on the same ground, so to speak. The dinner is a consummation devoutly to be wished, the culmination of everything — more valuable, even, than the defence itself.

It will be a relief to leave this department, Charlotte thinks, to start over some place new. The last grad-student party Charlotte attended, a woman cornered her in the kitchen: "Oh, you know how people talk, and for the whole two years since you arrived, everyone's been wondering 'How does she do it? How does she do it?'" Charlotte smiled at first, thinking this a compliment. How does she do it? It's not easy — single motherhood, the course work, the research — and here she is, with the grades, the defence, her beautiful daughter bringing home glowing report cards, reading above grade level ... It wasn't until Charlotte got home late that night that she understood: the woman was asking not how she does it, but how she pays for it. The other stuff doesn't count, the hard work, the discipline, the sacrifice: null and void. All they want to know is how she pays for it.

So yes, Charlotte decides, there will be a post-convocation party, but no grad students, just family, friends, and faculty. Lots of faculty, maybe a few sessionals.


Charlotte's mother left this world with desperation and style in equal measure. Her suicide was legendary, a work of vengeful art. Thoughtfully arranged so that the body would be found by a non-relative, the housekeeper. The detailed instructions for the funeral written in flowing Bishop Strachan longhand, fountain pen, peacock-blue ink. The menu (artful pepper and artichoke salad, grilled salmon, chocolate mousse), the orchestra (Eric Friedenberg), the music (Sinatra tunes from the fifties, mostly, with one exception), the order of business (eulogies by non-family only, readings from the Bible for the children). The finishing touch was the insistence that Charlotte's father and his mistress take the dance floor first, as at a wedding, to the strains of "Proud Mary." Everyone knows it's bad form to speak ill of the dead, but disobey them? Charlotte's mother put it to the test, and everyone on the guest list showed, the major players at least, their faces taut and grey, their shoulders clenched with shame and duty. The women who'd dropped Charlotte's mom the moment her sanctified tie to power was cut; the business cronies who'd turned a blind eye. They scarfed back the food and drink, all of it pre-charged to her ex-husband's account. And Charlotte's father and his ladyfriend danced, stiffly, ludicrously.

Charlotte remains grateful that she did not find her mother, did not see her draped across the back seat of the SEL 650, beautifully made up, dressed in a peach peignoir. A bottle of pills backed up the kindness of the idling motor of the Mercedes, even though it had just been tuned and filled. With premium.

Outside the funeral home, the mother's best friend sobbed tears and mascara indelibly onto the shoulder of Charlotte's Jones New York suit. "I can't understand it, the waste, an eyelift just three weeks ago." The divorce settlement — townhouse and furnishings, jewellery, art, annuity — not generous, but just this side of a lawsuit, was signed over in entirety to Charlotte.

"It never fails, at all those parties of yours," Charlotte once said to her mother, the last time they ever got drunk together, "the way the dance floor fills when the band strikes up 'Proud Mary.'"

Over dessert and coffee, Jake tells a story about an argument he had with a grad student about her interpretation of *The Changeling*, and how Jake said to this girl, "'You just don't seem to have a grip on the moral universe of this play,' and she looked at me like I'd said, I don't know, 'Fuck your mother' or something."

Stella puts her hand on his shoulder and says, "Hon, using the phrase 'moral universe' in 1994 *is* like saying 'fuck your mother.' The concept of any kind of mutually agreed-upon morality is tainted with patriarchal hegemony, the ideology of the dominant culture."

"Look, all I said to her was 'Beatrice-Joanna ain't no Doris Day, and when she hires Antonio to kill a guy for her, and then acts surprised when he asks for ass instead of cash, I find her disingenuous. She had to have known that's what he wanted——'"

"Jake, if you ask somebody to fix your car, or help you avoid income tax, you don't automatically bend over and spread when he comes to collect, do you?"

"Jesus, Stella, it's not the same thing——"

"Why not? Because she's a woman? Why is sex her only currency? She offered him money."

Jake takes a huge slug of wine, and flings himself back on the couch. "I for one sincerely look forward to the day when all academic feminists can be shot on sight with impunity."

Stella smiles at him tenderly. "Present company excepted, I presume."

Charlotte has lost the drift momentarily, still reeling from hearing the word "fuck" come out of Stella's mouth.

"Help me out here, Charlotte, you're under thirty——"

"Huh? Oh. Just over."

"Just over, then. What can I do? I'm white, I'm old, I'm a guy. The only thing I've got going for me in these dangerous times is that I'm not dead, yet. God, you've got a fighting chance and at least you're a woman and——" And then there's the child. Jake's sudden blush is so endearing, so delicious, that neither woman can make a move to rescue him from it. But Maya does, calling from the den, "Jake, *The Simpsons* is on!", leaving Stella and Charlotte to rehash the events of the defence one more time.

The guests are still out front, she can hear the slam of car doors, and already she is awash, she is wild with wondering — What did they think, what are they saying? How wonderful Charlotte's loyalty to her late mother; what a dedicated mother Charlotte is herself; how interesting that she doesn't drink; and isn't her child charming, articulate, adult beyond her ten years — that sweet question Maya asked about *The Simpsons*. Who fathered this dark-skinned child? Where is he? Charlotte recognizes this wildness as desire — to be loved, appreciated, understood, recognized. Seen. She is familiar with certain kinds of desire, but this is new. Maya calls from her room, it's time for a snuggle, but Charlotte is too high. She calls, "Just a sec." She needs more time to savour the conversation, to let it all sink in. To understand how badly she has wanted this evening; to replay Stella's self-deprecating maternal tales; to picture Stella on the couch, clutching a glass of wine and laughing. Jake looking shy. Maya primly passing a bowl of mixed nuts, proud of herself.

Is Stella saying, "I never knew ..."? Is Jake saying "unusual girl"? All the anticipation Charlotte has been feeling about her date with the coffee-shop man, all that building lust and the *zzt* of circuits hooking themselves up again, all that is gone. Can one kind of desire utterly displace another?

"MO-OM."

"Coming," says Charlotte.

After Maya is asleep, and the kitchen is cleaned up, Charlotte reclines on her living-room couch, observing the smoke-plumed towers of downtown with detachment, and thinking: Stella. Teacher, mother, sister, kindred. Stella.

INTERLUDE: In the Car

"So you've unleashed another one," Jake says, humping into the passenger seat. They'd decided that Stella's measure of legal impairment was one glass below his. "Jesus, Stella, how can you live with yourself?"

"Not to mention that her proposal was refused twice and I had to go through the third draft line by line——"

"She's a strange one, with her piccaninny——"

"Jesus, Jake——"

"And how the hell does she do it? A single mother, a grad student in a townhouse like that? Did you see the art? That was a Buck Kerr above the couch, you know——"

"Not to mention the fact that I wrote the concluding paragraph for every damn chapter. The woman is incapable of reaching a conclusion——"

"I'm thinking of."

"What? Oh. Give me more."

"I'm thinking of Joan Didion."

"I know this ..."

"Novel."

"*Play It as It Lays?*"

"Nope, I'm giving it away now. Central character: Charlotte."

"Of course. *A Book of Common Prayer.*"

"And the line?"

"Give me a minute"

He fidgets. "Give up?"

"I don't know——"

"That's the first part."

"It is? Yes! 'I have never known anyone with so unexamined a life as Charlotte.'"

"Bingo. Allusion?"

"Aristotle? — 'The unexamined life is not worth living.'"

"Socrates. Pretty rusty, Stel, but it'll do."

This is their favourite game, their own version of "Name That Tune." After nearly two decades, the ties that bind them are mainly rags and tatters — of ideas, habits, notions. And this game. As Jake and Stella sit side by side in their car, the game reassures them, if only for the moment, that they still belong together.

## 2. Another Dinner

"I am driving out to The Projects to get laid." Charlotte says this out loud, pleased with herself. The Projects, in this part of the world anyway, is a new subdivision on a hillside west of the city. At the entrance, a billboard announces that walkout splits start at only $110,9! Long curving boulevards. Row on row on row of neat, gleaming dwellings, stacked three high like egg cartons. This is the place people come to when they walk out, split (or when someone walks out, splits, on them), to these bunkers, with grassless yards and unpoured driveways. The vinyl siding in white, eggshell, off white, hasn't yet lost its sheen. Spindly trees, wired to a standing position against the prairie winds and planted at carefully measured intervals, struggle upward on the boulevard.

Charlotte's eight-month abstinence has been instructive. She notices things more acutely now: how lust transforms the world, makes the lyrics of pop songs ache with meaning, reconnects the neural circuitry, awakens the animal self. The man she is going to is a good prospect, distant enough from his divorce to be over the worst bitterness, yet still eager to please. This will be their second date. The night they met for a drink, Charlotte said, "I'm celebrating tonight. I just defended my MA thesis." Ever since, he's used the word "consequently" as often as possible. Maybe it's the only four-syllable word he knows.

The evening goes smoothly: they have dinner, dessert, and are naked by ten — one thing Charlotte has learned very well is to allow a man to think he's the one doing the seducing. Strange, though — Charlotte thought that, after all this time, the mere weight of a man's body would transport her to the direst ecstasies. But no. In fact, it's a little boring at first. Oh, this again. Two minutes on the left nipple, two minutes on the right, a tickle between the legs, and then *whamwhamwham*. Do they all read the same manual or something?

And she's not at all sure she likes the way he says "pussy" all the time.

The first time Charlotte ever heard the word *pussy*, applied to the female anatomy at least, was when she was eight years old. Her parents were having a party, and though she'd been sent to bed hours before, she couldn't sleep, and padded down the hall in her nightie, to sit at the top of the stairs. Sometimes, at these parties, her mother would perch on top of the piano and sing "A Guy's a Guy" or "Mockingbird Hill," but this night, there were only the voices of the men in the corridor below. Charlotte's father was telling a joke— "So she comes back into the bar and the bartender says, 'Another case of Blue?' and the squaw says [and here his voice moved into a tight-lipped mutter], 'Naw,

gimme Molson Golden this time, Blue makes my pussy hurt.'"
The roar of laughter drifted up the stairs.

Maya's dad liked that word, too. She wonders if he even
knew how to read. Why is that, Charlotte wonders, why the
separation? "Go to the site of your oppression," Stella always
says. Stella says that the moment when you feel ashamed, in-
competent, inadequate, stupid — this is the moment to pay
attention to, you are at the site of your oppression and you
must go there — not cringe, not flinch, not slink away. Going
to the site of her oppression, Charlotte asks herself: Why separate the life of the mind from the life of the body, why one
woman at the desk and a different one in the bed (and on the
couch and the rug and in the shower and against that lovely
rough tree: where was that? who was that? Marvellous—). No,
Charlotte tells herself, concentrate.

She thinks about Stella. She thinks about Jake. Not bad-
looking, a little scruffy. The notion of sexual ambition comes
to Charlotte with a newness, a starkness, almost like a mark of
maturity. The notion is conceived as she reclines on a crisp new
couch still slick with Scotchguard, the notion gestates as she
watches a naked man move deftly about the room, adjusting
the lights, the candles, the stereo.

Midnight, and Charlotte sprawls, sated, on the imitation Per-
sian rug on the living-room floor. She really must think of getting home soon; the sitter might be waiting up. Charlotte's legs
are apart, and the Chinook that rattles through the venetians
feels like an angel's tongue. The man brings glasses of Perrier,
"How're ya doin'?" he says. Which means "How'm I doing?" of
course. "Perfect, wonderful," Charlotte says. Everything in his
house is brand new. This man has made a clean start. "I wanted
a kind of Cape Cod effect," he says. The sincerity of his faith in

the redemptive powers of decor makes her want to weep.

When Charlotte moved into her mother's townhouse, she found a stack of journals stuffed into a liquor-store box at the back of the closet. Charlotte opened the box that night in expectation of wonders, the *explication du texte,* the mystery of Charlotte's life held up to the light.

And there was nothing, not a whiff. Perfect veneer. July 1969, her mother — crazed and desperate — set fire to the bedroom curtains, and Charlotte, aged seven, called the fire department. No one else was home at the time. And, infuriatingly, the entries read: "A little cloudy and cooler today. Mrs. Petrovsky came and polished the silver." Or "Lunch at the Club today. Wore my red suit." November 1977, the time Charlotte escorted her mother to a clinic in Pennsylvania, the time her mother flipped out at the departure gate and had to be restrained, sedated. "The flight was a bit long. Charlotte had the chicken. I had the beef and thoroughly enjoyed it." That was all.

The man is moving inside her again — the jasmine-scented candles, Bryan Ferry on the stereo — the world liquefies, and he's saying that word again. *Pussy.* A second climax builds out of nowhere, begins from the inside, so slow and strong and full that it catches her up and she cries out the man's name, and God's. Bryan Ferry croons "More Than This" and Charlotte thinks:

*Yes, exactly, yes.*

And her next thought follows so quickly that it's almost simultaneous:

*And there's nothing less either.*

*PASSUS TWO*

<small>PARODY</small>
November 1995

*"I just want to see them," he said, whining like a child.*
*"See who?"*

Greta opens her door to a good-looking man in his late forties. Medium height; slim; longish grey hair, professionally styled. A slick smile. "Shall we start in the bedroom?" he says. The studio doesn't provide lingerie, but props are on offer. A long string of pearls, a single red rose, a marabou fan. He's delighted that Greta has a cat, a white one. *Beautiful, gorgeous,* he murmurs. He has loads of equipment — square black shoulder bags, shiny camera cases, three lights on metal stands with silky white umbrellas tilted at weird angles. While Greta changes in the bathroom, he sets up the lights. He must not like the colour of the bedspread because he decides to start in the bay window. *Gorgeous, beautiful,* he says, not looking at her but at the window. Greta has chosen a lacy black underwire and black satin tap pants. She throws her old terrycloth robe over top and pads out of the bathroom, feeling ridiculous. "Two secs," he says, crouching over his viewfinder, not turning around. Then he straightens, says "Right" and still without looking directly at her, says, "Greta" (he's used her name in every sentence he's uttered),

"Greta, if you're ready to disrobe now, please just sit over here."
She throws the robe on the closet floor, and walks to the window, feeling the gooseflesh blossom on her thighs. The first thing the photographer did when he came through the door was ask her to crank the thermostat up five degrees. As she seats herself carefully on the green velvet cushion, her knees pressed together, she hears a click and music wells up, sort of non-music actually — sinuous, sweet. The kind of rhythmic hump that signals the action in porno movies. The photographer spends ages adjusting the volume, fiddling with lights, glancing briefly, then murmuring instructions with his back to her, "Now lean back on the pillows, bring your right knee up. Lovely. Just inch that shoulder back. A little more. Fantastic ..."

Greta understands absolutely that if either of them so much as cracks a smile, the whole thing will collapse. This travesty must be performed with worshipful seriousness or it won't work.

*"I just what to see them," he said. "Please."*
*"See who?" I said, and then his hands were flying at the snap-buttons of my denim shirt and I saw that this man was giving me a gift, the desperate enactment of desire—*

The photographer finishes up just in time for her to get dressed and go pick up Zak for the concert. While they're sitting at the kitchen table, waiting for Zak to brush his teeth, she tells Stella about the boudoir photographs. "The best part was when he said, 'Greta, would you feel comfortable removing your brass-ee-air?'"

"Three syllables. Classy guy. It's the props that kill me," Stella says. "Christ, couldn't they have a little more imagination?

Like those chintzy fantasy rooms at West Edmonton Mall, fake leopard skin, Roman baths — good grief! Even our fantasies are tawdry these days——"

"Well, you can get live snakes, but it costs extra," Greta says. "It was lovely, though. Like that time when that guy, what's-his-name, he kept saying, 'I just want to see them.' I'm sure I told you that story——"

"Oh yeah! At our housewarming. Right after you got transferred here from the Coast. He was waiting for you in our bedroom when you came out of the can. And you said 'See who?' before you realized he was begging to see your tits. You told me, and I can't — Ralph, no Roy. He was a sessional from Anthropology, wasn't he?"

"Right, that was his name. But those six little words gave me years of getting up in the morning and looking in the mirror and saying, *Great God, girl, but that's a fine set you've got there!* Too bad I have to pay for it now, but hell. Worth every penny."

"All ready, Auntie Gretz," Zak says, and Stella grabs him for a hug as he passes. Gretz sees her standing at the back door, waving goodbye, absently hooking a thumb under her bra to haul it back into place. It was Gretz who'd convinced her to invest in a good underwire— "A feat of engineering, Stel. It'll gather all the available flesh and, hey presto, arrange it into two roughly breastlike objects in approximately the right place." But Greta should've known better than to send her out shopping unsupervised; Stella bought the wrong size, of course, and now the most striking feature on her chest is a thumb-shaped pucker front and centre in the fabric of the T-shirt of the day.

Zak hops and bops and claps his hands. He eats this stuff up. When they were heading out to the concert, Stella said, "He'll have a great time. My son is the quintessential postmodern kid — parody is his first language." The concert audience is a mix of fortyish yuppies with kids in tow, and teenagers and Gen X–ers who possibly wouldn't recognize parody if it came up and bit them on the ass.

The band swings into the grand finale, a medley of all the latest alternative screeches of solemn angst — every single one set to polka music. All that portentousness deflated, made ridiculous. Zak and Greta are still giggling and replaying their personal favourites all the way to the car.

"Thanks for taking me, Auntie Gretz. I probably could've talked Mom into it, but she wouldn't get the jokes."

"I know what you mean."

"All she ever listens to is CBC."

"Your mother lives in a world of her own. I've known her since high school, and the list of topics I can discuss with her is whittling down at an alarming rate."

"Like music."

"Right, unless it's opera or Gregorian chant."

"And TV."

"*Masterpiece Theatre* once a month, maybe?"

Zak tenderly strokes the lettering on his souvenir T-shirt. "She actually has Miranda convinced that watching sitcoms rots the brain. So Randa sits over there at Dad's, soaking up all those TGIF shows with this terrified look on her face, you can see her thinking: *ping, there goes another brain cell* ... We can't talk about Dad, either."

Or men in general, Greta thinks but doesn't say. "What else? Oh yes, clothes. Your mom and I used to live for clothes. We spent hours at Eaton's after school——"

"And now her idea of dressed up is a T-shirt with shoulder pads."

"Zak, you are a gem. And food. Either I'm on Jenny Craig or I'm talking about some new place I've been to, and you can see the smoke coming out of her ears———"

"I know, she just flipped out on us one night: 'How the hell can it be that my children have been to the Rainbow Bridge Café and I haven't?' She still cries a lot."

"She'll be okay, Zak. Hey, I just thought of another forbidden topic: movies. Remember that time I was over for Sunday dinner and your Mom got onto that movie about the German shepherd, Beethoven———"

"St. Bernard."

"Right, St. Bernard, and she's going on and on about how this movie is a thinly veiled, vicious attack on feminism, how the bad woman wears a suit and high heels and carries a briefcase, and the good woman stays home with her kids and makes cookies and cleans up dog pooh———

"You really pissed her off when you told her she was full of it."

"Zachary Morrison!"

"I'm in Grade four, it's the *lingua franca.*"

"You scare me, Zak. But in a good way."

"It's what I live for, Auntie Gretz," he says, smiling. "After all, I'm the son you're glad you never had."


Miranda is already in bed, and Zak says goodnight, leaving the two of them at the kitchen table. Stella pours the wine. Glancing over her shoulder to make sure the children's lights are out, she whispers, "Miranda said something interesting when they got home from Jake's the other night. I asked my usual 'How was your weekend, hon?' and she said, 'Okay, but I really miss Maya.'"

The animation on Stella's drawn face makes Greta's heart ache. This is probably the best thing that's happened to her in months, this paltry little rag of comeuppance. Stella looks like shit these days, hollow-eyed and greyish. Her baggy sweatshirts and wrinkled jeans make Greta nostalgic for the days when Stella at least wore polyester print skirts, elastic waist, from the Bay, with acrylic pullovers, dark tights, and penny loafers. Greta sighs, "So, you figure that Charlotte and Jake have broken up?"

"Maybe, could be."

"Has he changed his phone number?"

"No, but they weren't living together anyway. The kids haven't mentioned Charlotte much lately, but I never ask direct questions either. One time, they came home from their dad's place and said, 'Oh, it was Charlotte's birthday and we had a cake,' and the only safe thing I could think of was, 'That's nice. Was it chocolate?'"

"So if they have broken up ..."

"I don't know ... Justice. Vengeance. Wasting diseases." Stella refills her glass and lights another smoke. "Did I ever tell you that I wrote the concluding paragraph for every damn chapter of her stupid thesis?"

"I believe you've mentioned that, yes."

Stella drops her head into her hands. "Jesus. You know what I really hate about this? I mean, I knew Jake was a liar: he lied to his mother and his friends and his students. Why the hell did I think he wouldn't lie to me? How could I have been so stupid?"

"Well, the guy was good, you've got to admit. And maybe at some level you just didn't *want* to know."

"Mention my inner child and I'll kill you." Stella's grin is terrible.

"Hadn't crossed my mind, I swear."

"But Gretz, it's like something in me has just *turned*. It's like, okay — the other day, in the department lounge, I hear myself telling this Amusing Anecdote. About a temporary nanny I hired once, years ago, when Danita had to go back to the Philippines for a funeral. This temp was a fucking disaster, lasted three days and I fired her. Thick as a post, and ugly too. I came home the third day and she fluttered up to me and said, 'Oh, the funniest thing happened today, I lost the baby!' *'You what?'* I said. And I swear, she *giggled*; she said, 'Oh, I set her down in the Kanga Rocka Roo seat and then I forgot where I put her. I had to call Zak to help me look. Found her in the laundry room, on top of the dryer. She was fast asleep. Such a little sweetie.'"

"She told you *that?*"

"She thought I'd find it as funny as she did. Actually, one of her references phoned back after I'd already fired her and told me this story that made me think I was lucky to get rid of her before she 'forgot' the kids at a bus stop or left them outside the Money Mart in a running car while attempting to cash a forged cheque. But you know what was the worst, Gretz? What she wore to the interview. That's the story I told in the lounge. I saw myself sitting there, telling them what Raylene wore to her interview. Gretz, she was wearing a cocktail-party dress. A Kmart abortion of a cocktail-party dress, Gretz, cheap shiny fabric made entirely from petroleum products, vomit green with gold flecks like an Arborite countertop, and her big boobs flopping around inside, and this clump of fabric all gathered up on one hip, tightened over her loose belly and sort of jouncing on her big doughy thighs ... Jesus." Stella has started to cry. "All these years, I never told anybody about that dress. I figured it was like this one little kindness I could do her, one little recompense for being dealt a really shitty hand. And I saw myself sitting there, making her into an amusement like that, and I just——"

Greta lays a hand on Stella's arm. "You're still the same person."

"No, I'm not. I'm shit. Like everybody. Like them."

"Stel, you've always wanted the thing itself — but you know, maybe there is no thing itself. Maybe parody is all we can ask for, an approach to the thing itself, a resemblance. Do you know what I mean? It's like Weird Al's version of that Nirvana song.

Beats hell out of the original, as far as I'm concerned. You wanted to respect that woman, you tried. It's good enough. It has to be."

Greta finishes her wine and sets the glass on the table. "Remember those pictographs on the bathroom doors at the student union. First-year university?"

"Those what?" Stella snuffles unbecomingly.

"Somebody liberated the washrooms, went around to all those little figures wearing pants or a skirt, and painted them over from the navel down."

"Oh yeah," Stella says, "I always used to crack the door an inch and check for a urinal before I went in."

"Right. A worthy idea in principle but a few little wrinkles in practice. Like hiring a nanny so you can work. It presents practical problems you can't foresee."

Stella sighs, "Remember how John Lennon talks about fucking peasants in 'Working Class Hero'? I've never figured out whether he's using 'fucking' as an adjective or a verb."

"Can't ask him now," Greta says, reaching for her jacket.

Stella manages a thin smile. "God, Gretz, you should've seen that dress."

In the car on the way home, after midnight, Greta makes a mental note to buy Stella a pair of Gilda Marx leggings for Christmas. And a really good cotton shirt to wear over top — royal blue maybe. Or cerise.

Like the dress Charlotte was wearing in that photograph. A photograph which was displayed very briefly on Stella's mantel. Charlotte's dress was a deep cerise, high quality — Rouie maybe, or J.G. Hook. Flattering cut, a classic; it would last for years, properly accessorized. Greta has an eye for such things. The photo is long gone now, of course. Probably mutilated and tortured, the frame stomped, the photo scorched with flames from a Bic lighter.

The picture was taken at a cocktail party given by Charlotte to celebrate her convocation, two months after her defence. "A catered event — a grad student, can you feature it?" Stella had said to Gretz a few days later, showing her the pewter-framed photo and thank-you card that read: "I share this success with you." In the photograph, Stella, dressed carelessly in a white T-shirt and pale floral skirt, stands between Charlotte, in her cerise dress, and Jake, sporting his characteristic black scowl. Stella is grinning, her arms stretched around their shoulders; Charlotte's left arm and Jake's right are invisible behind her back.

Greta fiddles with the radio dial, and finds the alternative rock station. The singer screams about his rage, but all she can hear is its parody, jouncing happily along to a polka beat. She switches the radio off, and the photographer's voice drifts into her consciousness, a soft breath in her ear — *Lovely, oh that's great, beautiful.*

And then she hears Jake's voice jump the decades, as the sounds of the housewarming party hum below their feet: *Please, I just want to see them, oh lovely, oh.*

*PASSUS THREE*

Stigmata
July 1996

Louise had an absolutely fascinating experience this summer. She spent five days with a man. It was interesting. There were a couple of things she noticed.

She and Jake have known each other more than half their lives. Jake pointed this out to her, the night that he and his children arrived at the cabin. He said, "Remember that time we did it on the floor of Crookshank's office?"

Louise had forgotten that time. She remembered the time before that, though, in the mountains. A tram ride up Grouse Mountain, the two of them, eighteen and nervous and swaggering, searching among the rocks for a congenial patch of ground. Afterwards, Louise's underpants rolled away down the hill, caught by a puff of ocean breeze, and Jake chased after them, bareassed, giggling. They nearly missed the last tram down the mountain.

Haphazard lovers but always friends, the two of them. They got married the same year. Louise had never liked Stella; too prickly, too mouthy, too pleased with herself. Jake didn't like Louise's husband either — nobody's ever good enough for one's dearest friends. Anyhow, Jake's divorced now and so is Louise. He has two kids and so does she. Jake left his wife for a younger woman. Louise's husband did that too. Jake's younger woman dumped him within two years. Same thing happened to Louise's husband: around eighteen months, actually.

So Louise just spent five days with a man and she made several observations. Things men say, things they do.

She noticed that men throw their weight around. They do not make their beds. They do not tiptoe if they are the first to get up in the morning — no, they rattle and clatter and sing. They do not negotiate with children. They make absurd teasing jokes at which their kids laugh with dutiful boredom. Men do not ask permission to go out. Every day that he was there, Jake would just disappear for a while, sometimes for hours, without telling anyone where he was going or when he'd be back. He did not ask Louise to mind his children in his absence; he just assumed she would. As of course, she did — wiping noses, dishing up KD, applying Band-Aids and sunscreen, nagging about life-jackets. When Jake returned, he would relate his adventures and everyone was expected to pay attention.

She remarked that men don't watch what they say, as when Jake disparaged a writer by saying "He should have been a journalist" — apparently forgetting how Louise earns a living.

Louise also noted a marked fondness for numbers in male speech. Jake told her how many buffalo they saw on the way there (at least sixty), how many hours they drove (eleven), and what time he got everyone up in the morning for the trip (five-thirty). One evening, he told her how many times his former girlfriend came in a single lovemaking session (four).

Men have phrases that they use. Such as "She's a wonderful mother ...," leaving the word "but" seen but not heard, like a Victorian child. And then there's "The marriage was over," with the idea of "anyway," the idea of "so therefore" unsaid but implied.

Louise noticed, too, what men don't say. She observed that sometimes, when you speak to men, they do not respond. This usually happens when they are reading the paper.

Louise wondered whether, during their holiday together,

she and Jake would make love. She had forgotten the floor of
their English professor's office, but she remembered a splintery
log-cabin floor in Manitoba, the two of them wild on tequila
shooters and Thai sticks and moonlight. Louise hasn't been
around men too much in the past few years and she thought it
might be nice. A blanket on the ground in the thicket near the
cabin, under the stars, while the children slept in their bunks,
dreaming their sweet inexplicable dreams and blossoming with
swimmer's itch.

Nothing like that happened though. The first two nights
were cool and cloudy, and, on the third, Louise got sick. Nau-
sea; flashes of fever; a hard ache in her chest, right in the solar
plexus. As if the stigmata were travelling right through her body.
She slept poorly that night, kept thrashing and twisting in her
mummy bag until it was damp with sweat. After midnight,
Louise got up and wandered down to the lake, alarmed to find
herself hunched below the full moon, shaken with sobs. Muttering "Not like this, not this, no."

Louise had first noticed it, the stigmata, the day Jake and
his kids arrived, but she never got around to showing it to him.
There were a lot of things she'd looked forward to talking to
him about, actually, but the time just never seemed right. That
third day was her eldest's tenth birthday, and Louise wanted to
tell Jake how it feels to have been a mother for a decade. She
wanted to say, "I weaned her at thirteen months, and went to
Ottawa on assignment. How I luxuriated in that room at the
Lord Elgin, you'd think I'd won the lottery. And, the craziest
thing, I just fixated on what a treat it would be to leave my
toiletry bag open on the bathroom floor. A toxic dump of
Tylenols and shampoos and toners, just left in a heap — small
carelessness, it's what you really miss. And Jake, I couldn't do it.
Every time I walked past the bathroom door, my heart just
squeezed, this irrational panic — and while I was doing inter-
views, and when I slept, I dreamt her little mouth ringed with a

fatal slug of Estée Lauder wrinkle-defence lotion. So, the second night, I got up and slammed the toiletry bag onto the counter, pulled the zip so hard it broke, and just cried and cried. I don't think men *carry* their kids like that. I'd come all this way, but I still had this ghost child riding my hip ..."

Now that Louise thinks about it, there were quite a few things she didn't get around to telling Jake. As if something was there that they just couldn't break through. To give him credit, Jake wasn't in the best shape either — getting asked to leave the English Department, and then what's-her-name dumping him. The word is that she's in a doctoral program out East, bonking her present supervisor, of course. Jake said, "I really think she has perfected a kind of Zen detachment; she has no interest in the outcome." He said this so blind to his own pain that Louise ached for him, Jake, her old friend.

All the same, Louise found it an interesting five days. Men. They say the darnedest things. "She's a wonderful mother." (Yeah right, as if mothering is easy, and being a push-button tart is the real challenge.) And "The marriage was over." (Yes, but did you think to mention that to your wife, first?)

So Louise never did get around to showing Jake her stigmata. It was a heart-shaped patch of sunburn on her back. A perfect heart, no kidding. The size of her fist. At first she blamed her daughter, thinking damn lazy kid must've missed a spot when she spread the sunscreen, but no, it couldn't be, the shape was too perfect, a perfect symmetrical heart in the middle of her back, a little to one side. The stigmata had faded by the time Jake left, but the ache in Louise's chest lingered for a couple of days.

*PASSUS FOUR*

COTTAGE
1996/1997

*Maybe it was the letter she couldn't bring herself to throw away. It was dated March 15, 1996:*

*To: Diana Crossfield*
*From: Alvin Shaw, Head, Department of English*
*Thank you for your application for the tenure-stream position in Contemporary World Literatures. Despite your excellent teaching record and long service to this department as a sessional instructor, I regret to inform you that you were not among those shortlisted for an interview.*

*The handwritten postscript reads,*
    *I am so sorry about this, Di.*
    *Best, Al*

It's a three-hour drive from the city to the cottage, and the first thing Diana does when she arrives is check to make sure everything is still there. Soft, worn bedsheets patterned with purple roses, artfully hand-mended by a Polish cleaning woman they had when she was little. Maria Fiedorwicz — her name was the first long word Diana ever learned to spell. The one remaining mug from Mother's trousseau. Crocheted doilies on the arms of faded chairs. The frayed couch still redolent with the farts of a brindled boxer who died before her sons — now aged fifteen — were born.

Diana needs things to be the same, here. Exactly as they have been forever. A thank-you note in the desk drawer, from distant cousins in Chicago who visited on their way to Expo 86. The desk itself, which had belonged to Diana's great-grand-mother. The Sorry! game missing half the cards and all but three playing pieces. Fireplace bellows patched with duct tape. Tubes of Neosporin long past expiry dates resting beside an eyelash curler spotted with rust. These objects comfort her, give her hope. Of what, she couldn't say.

Bill and the boys are having their after-lunch siesta, but Diana is out on the dock. The lakeshore's unusually quiet today — some mysterious entomological holocaust has occurred and, at this moment, the lake is scummed over with shiny black slicks composed entirely of the lifeless bodies of thousands, possibly millions, of small insects. It'll take a few days of strong wind to blow all the corpses up onto the beach, so nobody's swimming right now. As she lies on her stomach, propped up on elbows, reading, she hears a mother duck calling softly to her brood. The duck glides up to the beach with a clutch of young — they are maybe six weeks old, mottled brown-and-white backs, glistening feathers — common merganser, prob-ably. The mother is a regally uniform chocolate brown, eyes and bill to match. The little family feasts on the insect bodies, burbling and snorting with pleasure. The clattering of their bills sounds like someone flipping through the pages of an old book. At last — once again — (always), Diana is glad that she's here.

For her, the only good thing about coming in August in-stead of July is the garden, and the fact that she gets to miss that godawful Annual Meeting. Someone left a copy of the minutes on the kitchen table. She never reads the thing, but Bill said something about a legal problem between the locals and the Cottagers' Association. *Let the others worry about it,* Diana thinks; *I'm on holiday.*

*Maybe it was the student giving a presentation on Nadine Gordimer's* July's People, *the African student who asked, "Why should I care about the views of this petty white woman?" He spat the words out, his anger pushing at Diana, sitting attentively with the other students, her pen poised to assign him a grade. Diana appreciates his entitlement but chafes at her own exclusion. Is there no place for petty white women in this problem? And what defines her pettiness? The fact that she's white? The fact that she's female? Both?*

In October, the meadow out behind the cottage is golden, the grass so dry it crackles. Diana and her family are careful with fires and, for a change, wear their life-jackets in the canoe. The water is still open, of course, and will be till just before Christmas. No fall colours here; the forest is evergreen. They walk, read, sit before the fire. And eat too much. That's what they came for.

Bill tries to understand, but the politics are so different at the Art College — he was hired, tenure stream, right out of Melbourne. He says, "You're too long in the tooth, my dear, as Richard Burton once said to Elizabeth Taylor. That's all. No reflection on your skills, just the way the world is these days. Besides, it's not like we need the money."

The two of them take a walk while the turkey hisses in the oven, the boys having solemnly sworn that the concept of basting is well within their culinary grasp. On the hillside above the trail to Crater Lake, they find the leg of a deer, the greyish hide and hoof still perfectly intact, the bone jaggedly cracked just above the knee joint.

"Damned poachers," Bill says.

*Maybe it was the successively more sombre and hostile grad students, like the one who interrupted Diana in mid-anecdote to observe, "Have you ever noticed how many sports metaphors you use?" Maybe it was wardrobe, Diana learning to dress down. No more tailored floral shirtwaists from the Mirror Room. No more Ports corduroy. Eventually Tabi Casuals seemed like overdressing. Bill eventually suggested sackcloth and ashes.*

A dusting of November snow makes the grass shimmer and whisper; the lake maintains its pristine reserve, its cold greenblue. No ice yet — a mild winter. On her walk this morning, she nearly stumbled over three yearling whitetails. Two turned and ran, but the one closest the road froze, locked a proud gaze till Diana's eyes watered. The creature's marvellous, heartbreaking dignity in the face of threat, of fear.

Every time she comes here, she brings the weight of every other time. A chaste first kiss, at age fourteen, from Hal Neilson, as they sat side by side on the dock. Skinnydipping with her sister in a shimmering ribbon of moonlight on her seventeenth birthday. Honeymooning with Bill — they made love out on the deck on a June day, the strangeness of hot sun on the shy flesh between her legs. Walking the floor with Adam in her arms one Christmas, listening to his panicky wheeze and hard cough with terror in her heart. The remains of every pet she's ever owned scattered in the tall grass in the meadow beside the beaver pond. She's told Bill and the guys that's where she wants to be scattered too.

*Maybe it was that 304 seminar last term, the time Diana inter-ceded to say, "I'd like to move away, for a moment, from the ideo-logical aspects of the text and focus for a moment on its aesthetic qualities, and talk about what makes it beautiful, how it gives the reader pleasure——"*

*"But, Professor Crossfield," said the young woman with the strawberry-blonde dreadlocks and two nose rings, "if the aesthetic is viewed as an elitist construct, as Borchevsky has pointed out, then doesn't discussion of such things as image and metaphor be-come an ideological problem in itself?"*

On Christmas Eve, Diana glances out the window, seeing only the profound blackness of a winter night in the mountains, but she knows what lies out there in the dark, as well as she knows the faces of her own children: Old Man Mountain, Curly's Peak, Cougar, the Brass Knuckle, the stony hills with their hidden lakes below, and the pine forest below that. This place that be-longs only to grizzly, bald eagle, cougar, deer, coyote. How des-perately she needs these mountains; how desperately she needs their innocence.

She says to her husband, "The ice isn't in yet. Isn't that strange? It almost always freezes up by Christmas. I remember one year when a sudden freeze came before the first snow. The lake was like a sheet of glass. We skated all the way down to the south end and back. Stones sparkling clear underneath, zip-ping by beneath my feet. It made me dizzy."

The next morning, when Diana goes for her walk, she lifts

her eyes to the hills whence comes her comfort, and imagines that she sees flashes of bright colour — the red and purple hiking jackets of cottagers, jackets that let the sweat out and keep the water off, jackets with a zillion concealed pockets, and Mountain Equipment Co-op labels. She thinks she sees cottagers waving gaily from hilltops and woods, appropriating every branch of every tree, claiming every note of birdsong.

*Maybe it was going to a keynote address by the famous Anunda Borchevsky at a conference called "Naked Dominance: Anxieties of the Margins." The woman wandered on stage: maroon buzz cut; blue fingernails; black lips; and a full-skirted square-dance dress, bright red with yellow rickrack. She stepped up to the lectern and said, "For every unacknowledged rapture, there is a proportional hegemony." Everyone in the auditorium scribbled this down, and the speaker paused while they did. Then she said, "For every unacknowledged hegemony, there is a proportional rapture." Heads bent, pens scraped. Borchevsky had no notes — she rambled incoherently, and showed a couple of murky slides of the contents of her bedroom closet, and a video of a performance artist dressed as a penis, dancing and singing a song about phallogocentrism. Several times, the speaker asked the moderator, "How much time do I have left?" Eventually, the keynote address trailed off into barely audible muttering, and the moderator suggested, "Perhaps we could have questions now." There was a long silence, a lot of stirring in chairs and checking of notes. Diana raised her hand. "I'm not sure I understand the relevance of the video you showed to your point about hegemonies. Could you elaborate?"*

*The speaker smiled and said, "What would be the point of that? Any other questions?"*

*Maybe it was after Borchevsky's talk, when Diana asked a colleague what she thought of the talk: "Very interesting."*

*"What point do you think she was making?"*

*"Well, there was just so much there. I'd really have to think about it," Diana's colleague said, her eyes searching the corridor. "Excuse me, I really must——"*

*Diana persisted, "But she didn't answer my question!"*

*"Jesus, Diana, haven't you ever heard of deconstruction?"*

A February thaw, then a sudden freeze. The lake, a sheet of glass; each individual pebble shining, frozen deep, at the scalloped edges of the ice, where the trees have kept the snow off. The weather, glorious; Diana sunbathed on the deck this morning, then cross-countried down to the south end, singing to the rhythmic scrape of her skis. Every once in a while, the ice groaned as it shifted in the sun, like a mythical beast roaring out a warning. Year after year, she has to talk herself into believing that the ice will support her weight, and, year after year, she gathers the courage to ski as far as the point only to find the ice already bearing the weight of dozens of ice fishermen with rickety wooden shacks and crackling bonfires, as well as several snowmobiles and pickup trucks. She wishes Bill and the kids were here to see this day.

The nights are cold, and she bundles up in a plaid blanket on the deck to watch the stars. A pack of coyotes in the pasture behind are watching too, and they set up their song circle, the delicious spooky howl of the pack gliding down the boat ramp to the still water and shimmering like a tambourine round the bay. Diana listens, listens, and then tilts back her head to howl with them: *I am fed to the teeth with apologizing.*

*Maybe it was Diana's student, the bright and funny Melissa O'Brien, a gem in undergrad — clear-headed, creative, exquisite close-reading skills. Melissa began grad school with great promise. But by the end of fall term, she looked unhinged, skeletal, pale with shame. At first, she'd slink into Diana's office, haunted, saying "I just don't understand ..." By winter term, Melissa avoided Diana, looked right through her at readings and lectures. At the annual grad-student conference in March, Melissa stood up to give a paper in which she cried and apologized publicly for being white, middle-class, and racist.*

Quite a few families here this Easter, a big crowd of Jeep Cherokees parked over at the other end of the bay. The Neilsons must be having a cocktail party tonight. To which Diana and her family are not invited, thank God.

Diana has never really fit. A chunky, strong figure of a woman, inclined to be sedentary. Diana's husband and their twins — they all match. They are bookish, suspiciously artsy. While the others here race about in a frenzy of healthful outdoor activity, Diana and her family can often be found sitting quietly on the deck, reading or sketching or listening to music. When the twins were only about two, Adam cried out, as they crested the hill and glimpsed the smooth green surface of the lake, "I think we live in a dream!" It became a family tradition; all these years, they wait for the car to crest that last rise, wait for the first glimpse of that still green water, and then cry in unison, "I think we live in a dream."

*Maybe it was sitting down one night to compose her letter of resignation, then realizing that, after twelve years, none was required. She has no contract, she has no benefits, she has no pension. If she does not send her usual letter of application in April, her name will simply not appear on the list of candidates for the appointments committee in May, nor on the list of this year's sessional instructors in June. It's as simple as that.*

It's the second evening of Diana's annual women's weekend, held at the cottage the last week in April, to celebrate the end of winter term. She and Stella take a walk after dinner. Though she has worked with most of these women for more than a decade, it's only Stella she can trust: "So I'm chatting in the coffee room with the new hire, and she's in the throes of a childcare crisis, so I say, 'Oh, I remember once what a panic I was in when our nanny quit on us, it was a nightmare—' and this woman just looks at me and says, 'I wouldn't — I mean, I don't ... have ... a *nanny*.'"

"Don't worry." Stella smirks. "She will the first time her kid gets chicken pox or Hib flu and can't go to daycare for ten days——"

"And then last month, in front of the whole class, my own TA questions my inclusion of Blake's 'Little Black Boy' on the syllabus. Stella, I've always taught that poem as an antiracist polemic! I couldn't even find the words to defend myself, I was speechless, humiliated——"

"Di, you're a born teacher. Intellectual fashions come and go. Hell, I just take what I can use from all that *nouveau* theory. I fake it half the time."

"I can't fake it any more. After classes ended, I was 'invited' to do some volunteer work with the Persons of Colour Collective. The head co-signed the letter, for Chrissake. I stand for committees and don't get elected. My grant proposals get turned down. Face it, Stel, I'm a pariah. I just don't fit any more——"

A Rocky Mountain bluebird flashes by them, its plumage a

beyond-words shimmering sky blue. There's such a tiny window of opportunity to see them; a week or two at most every spring, as they rest on their way north. "Look!" Diana says. "Isn't that something? Have you ever seen anything so blue, except in your dreams?"

*Maybe it was that birthday dinner for Stella two weeks later, at the Greek restaurant. Ten women at a round table, shouting stories over shrilling bouzouki music. Diana had met the legendary Gretz only once or twice before, and sat transfixed by this lively, impossibly well-groomed woman across the table. Gretz was telling a story about how, in a meeting with an important client from Hong Kong, she was suddenly struck by his uncanny resemblance to the lover in* The Lover, *and was embarrassed to find herself nearly swooning with lust while trying to present a campaign proposal.*

*Stella laughed and turned to Diana. "I know what you mean about that guy, we saw that film out at the cottage a few weeks ago——"*

*Gretz, still riding the mirth of her story, oblivious really, crowed, "Oh, I've heard about* that *place. They call it a cottage? A palace more like, or a fortress——" Gretz stopped abruptly as if she'd been kicked below the table——*

*"Did I say something?" Stella's eyes locked on Diana's. "Aw, Di. Geez. I'm sorry——"*

*"Forget it," Diana said, forking a vine leaf into her mouth. "Don't you just love the lemony taste of these? And the vine leaves are so tender! Usually they're tough as shoe leather."*

*After the appetizer plates were taken away, Diana excused herself to a ladies' room lavish with red-flocked wallpaper and warning signs about the potentially fatal consequences of using the linen-towel dispenser incorrectly. Diana leaned her hands on the vanity so heavily that the counter's edge dug deep red troughs in her palms.*

*She gazed at her reflection and understood finally, absolutely, that mere goodwill is insufficient. That she is a freak, a curiosity. No one's fault, really, just an inescapable fact of her existence.*

At the 1997 annual meeting of the Cottagers' Association, a tempest. The locals apparently are up in arms, demanding beach access. They've gotten to the offspring of the farmer from whom the association, the parents and grandparents of the current cottagers, bought this property a few years after the war. Yes, the price sounds absurdly low now. It was a fair price at the time, but the lawyers of the farmer's grandchildren don't think so. Compensation, access, democracy, justice.

Hal Neilson, now a partner in his father's law firm, speaks eloquently, movingly — practised at turning offence and terror into logical argument. He warns of Eden destroyed, the roar of jet skis and big power boats shattering this pristine peace that their ancestors bought and paid for nearly fifty years ago. Destroying this priceless refuge from the pressures of modern life, this miracle of a private mountain lake.

Bill and Diana trudge home without speaking, as barn swallows reel orange/blue above their heads. Bill says, quietly, "I've always wanted to try my hand at camping."

All Diana can think of to say is "I think we live in a dream. I think we always have."

That night, Diana can't sleep, so she wanders outside, sits cross-legged on the dock. A crisp, clear night — a riot of stars, the lake so still that the preening of a duck half a mile away creates chatty ripples against the wood beneath her. She listens.

Loons call out to each other as the ripples subside. Then, the silence is huge.

Diana goes back inside the cottage, finds a piece of paper and a pen, and sits down at the desk that once belonged to her great-grandmother. She writes:

*July 3, 1997:*
*I can see no place for myself. Please accept my resignation.*

Diana has no one to send this letter to, so she puts it in an unsealed envelope and places it gently in the drawer of the old desk that has sat in this corner of the cottage since before she was born.

*PASSUS FIVE*

Dirty
Winter 1997

Angela bends over the figure of what once had been a man. She can see traces, very faint, of the person who once inhabited this shell — the thick wavy hair would have been dark and lustrous. The ice-blue eyes, so vivid now in the gaunt face, would have snapped with laughter and intelligence. The dying of these young men takes so long, their still-vital hearts not seeming to understand that it's over now, that struggle is pointless.

Angela's new patient has chosen to die at home, in the care of his cousin Greg. They grew up together in a small town on the prairies — "Two dreaming boys," Greg says. "I didn't even know he was gay, didn't even know what gay was, but we were closer than brothers, always have been."

Greg leaves for work when Angela arrives in the morning, and she bathes and changes the patient, treats his lesions, does meds, calls the doctors, washes dishes — just whatever needs doing. The patient's dementia is advanced; he has Kaposi's sarcoma, he has pneumonia, and he requires spoonfeeding. Even though she's used to terminal cases, this man strikes her heart. He's only forty-two, but he looks eighty. Ashen-faced, pockmarked with open sores, the skin on his toes peeling away. He gasps, his jaw works frantically, ceaselessly; his eyes are feverbright with terror. His thin arm flails at her as she stands at the bedside, and she doesn't know whether this means he wants her to go away or to come closer. He is no longer able to speak. While the patient sleeps, she prowls his house, Victorian gingerbread, gorgeously renovated, full of antiques and paintings.

Those seven weeks changed everything. It makes Angela think of the first time her children were invited to a birthday party at Chuck E. Cheese. She had run ahead to hand over the gift and arrange pickup time, and when she turned back, there, clinging to Nigel's hands, were their two little girls — hair curled and pinned back with beribboned barrettes, party clothes rustling with newness — and on their little faces a holiness, an unwavering certainty of wonders, of delights beyond imagining.

The magic held for them that afternoon. Never mind the bubblegum wads under tables, the chintzy prizes that break before you get them home, the ratty carpet sticky with spilled pop.... For a moment, they possessed paradise. And once, for a few weeks, so did Angela.

The patient was an artist, and, though the Pre-Raphaelite prints appealed to her at first, in time she was drawn to the paintings he'd done himself. The pictures were sort of ordinary-looking at first, just everyday objects. A cracked teacup. An old T-shirt hanging on the back of a chair. A pair of gardening gloves on a table, with clots of earth still clinging to the fingers, almost luminous in a shaft of sunlight. Angela had never really looked at paintings before, but she began to like whatever these were saying, and to like the man who'd made them. Each day, she chose a different painting to hang on the wall in his room, wanting this beauty he'd made to be the first thing he saw when he woke up.

One day she was staring at that T-shirt while the patient slept and she understood that the paintings were about desire.

When she was a little girl, Angela and her cousins used to sneak off to a stifling tent set up outside the family cottage, where they'd tell "D" stories. Their special code — little girls love their secrecies. "D" meant dirty. This was the fifties and their repertoire of dirty was limited. Getting "stripped" was the most dire thing they could imagine: it meant that a man takes off your clothes. The settings varied — a girl goes on a funhouse ride with a boy she doesn't know, a girl accepts a lift down to the store from a kindly old farmer — but the stories always ended the same way: "and then he stripped her."

The mention of the word *honeymoon* used to terrify Angela. It meant that a man would probably see her naked.

The change that occurred that winter is visible in snapshots. There's one, taken at her daughter's dance recital: Nigel took a couple of "Just mommy, because she looks so pretty today." And she did, then — it's the way her body inhabits space, the way the muscles of her face relax against the bones, the direct look of a woman who has a right to be here.

Six weeks later, the day before she told her husband: Their younger daughter's birthday party, ten screaming kids racing around the dining room, and poof, the old Angela back again: the baggy shirt, the grey skin, deep slashing lines around the mouth, and sagging shoulders. And the eyes....

Angela's husband, Nigel, is a PK, like her. A Preacher's Kid. Nigel was her lab partner in second-year Biology, and it was recognition at first sight. The excesses of the sixties were so terrifying, so embarrassing, that they rescued each other, wore each other like life-jackets. Safe sex. Angela said to her mother, "He's a good man, he'll be a good provider." She said to her cousins, "Nothing special, but a good guy. If I don't say yes now, in two or three years he might be gone."

They tried to please each other. They read books; they Tried New Things; they even rented a dirty movie, which turned her off sex for a month. Once, afterwards in bed, he touched her shoulder and said, "You know, Angie, not everybody has a high sex drive. It's okay, honey, I love you more than anything else in the world."

Nigel's old friend from grad school, Diana, came to town with her husband for a conference a few years back, and Nigel and Angela took them out to dinner. Most of Nigel's faculty pals just make Angela feel so dumb, but not Diana and Bill. He's Australian, and as they sat in the restaurant, a woman walked by, and Bill said, "*She's* dirty." *Shay's deah-tee.* Angela pestered him to tell her what that meant, but all he'd say was, "Dirty. Like Susan George in *Mandingo.*"

She vaguely recalled a wispy blonde. "But I've never seen *Mandingo.* You don't mean she needs a bath?"

Diana helped her out. "It means sexually available, or no, not even that — sexually self-aware, I guess."

"Oh," Angela said, baffled.

Walking home from the restaurant, the men up ahead talking department politics, Diana said, "You know how it gets in your second trimester, when you're just electric with lust. Sure, it's all just biomechanical, a suffusion of blood to the pelvis, but I got so red hot I was a public menace — that's dirty."

Angela was still trying to think of a response as Diana continued, "Friend of mine went through that phase big time with both her kids, and when I made some joke about how the second trimester can really revive a marriage, she just looked blank. She said, 'He didn't know about it; I didn't tell him.' And right then I knew those two were never going to last. I was right too."

This blitheness bothered Angela. "You and Bill don't know how lucky you are," she said. "Not everybody has what you have." It was the closest she'd ever come to telling another person — but then there were the men, waiting at the crosswalk to gather them back in to the circle, the brandy-scented laughter of old friends. Diana had time only to offer a look, and the matter was not spoken of again.

That painting. The sun-faded texture of the blue cotton, sweat stains on the collar, a dribble of coffee , a streak of paint — each fold and crease and shadow rendered with such worship, a devotion Angela could only imagine. She knew that the blue T-shirt had really existed once. That it had been worn by someone the artist loved more than his own life. She spent more time with those pictures each day. The earth on the gardening gloves just glowed; she could almost feel it between her fingers.

She read to the man in the bed too; his cousin said he liked Auden, so she read "Lay your sleeping head my love, human on my faithless arm" and "The day of his death was a dark cold day." One Monday morning, when she arrived and let herself in, Greg was sitting at the bedside. He wasn't dressed for work yet, looked like he hadn't slept or shaved or eaten all weekend.

"Angie," he said, "I don't think either of us can take much more of this." She moved toward them, crooning, "It's all right, his pain is under control. It's a matter of weeks, maybe even days," but the words sounded hollow. Then Angela did something she'd never done before. She just opened her arms to him, to them both. Words just failed.

*A lover's question: What part of my body do you like the best? He thinks, only for a moment, and says, "Your legs." He smiles. "Up in the air above my head."*

While the patient lay dying, Greg and Angela became lovers. They'd make love in the room down the hall. Each downward step — each new complication, tumour, infection — just raised the pitch of their loving higher. There came a point where Angela almost believed that, if they stopped making love, death would claim them too. While the patient slept fitfully, his caregivers tumbled and laughed together on an ornately carved oak bed with an antique mirror positioned just so. Once they stayed naked all day, and there was nothing about his body or hers that Angela didn't adore. There wasn't a fold or cranny that was not beautiful beyond all imagining; it was a transformation that was miraculous and yet oddly unsurprising, as if it were their due, all three of them. Greg said, "It seems unfair, him all alone and the two of us here. Do you think he hears us, do you think he knows?"

Angela answered, "If he does, I'm sure it pleases him, this energy, the pleasure — it fills up the whole house. It's like a feather bed for him, a balm...."

Dirty. When Angela was dirty, the world sang with congratulation, and benevolence seeped up through cracks in the sidewalk, the dishes washed themselves. She doesn't remember a single detail of domestic life through that whole seven weeks. She knows that she worked and cared for her children and slept beside her husband and went to the bathroom and did laundry, but she doesn't remember doing any of those things. She remembers feeling enthroned by pleasure, alive to the subtlest synaptic pulse, her nether parts a flower that described all the joy in the world.

The doctor ordered more and more morphine, and the patient gasped and struggled like a fish thrown up on a riverbank. Angela said to Greg, "The drug suppresses his breathing, it makes it terrible for him. You know him better than anyone. What do you think he would want?" They went against doctor's orders, halved the dose, then quartered it, then cut it down to an eighth, and the patient stilled, he quieted. Angela could see the relief and gratitude; this man was strong enough to withstand his own pain. She and Greg slept entwined; she couldn't imagine letting go of him. As if his touch was keeping her alive. Two days later, on a dark cold day, the patient died peacefully in his sleep. The lovers sensed the stillness and walked down the hall to the patient's room, holding hands. They stood for a moment, then Greg reached over and closed his cousin's eyes. Angela watched, still feeling the touch of those big gentle hands on her skin, and a rush ran through her, washed over her, watery fire, the blood visibly pulsing in her veins. The two of them sat with the body for half an hour, then made the necessary calls.

*A lover's question: He says, "And what part of my body do you like best?" No hesitation. "Your hands. Right there, heel of the hand in the soft flesh of my hip, generous fingertip circling my nipple, like that right there—"*

The night of the funeral, Angela stayed and helped clean up the glasses and ashtrays and Nanaimo-bar crumbs. Even though the evening was warm, she and Greg lit a fire. Because she'd said to him, "You know, this whole time we've never made love in front of the fire or in the Jacuzzi." So they did both of those things, maybe because they thought they were supposed to. But the hot water made her lightheaded and sick to her stomach, and the fire made the air around them dry, somehow unwelcoming. Over and over, the release gathered in her, then ebbed away. So strange to hear words of regret and apology, as if they were using a forgotten language. As she walked out the door of the gingerbread house, not shame itself but the merest notion of shame brushed past her, like a whisper, like a small insect that lights a moment and is gone.

Logistics became more difficult, the deceit more conscious, after the artist's death. Angela had a new patient, across town, and the only time available was the occasional weeknight after she'd dropped the kids at soccer practice, or lunch hour. Greg had always been single; he didn't understand why she couldn't just be there on a whim.

And then he made this stupid joke. She'd asked him about RRSPs, and he said, "If you keep asking me for financial advice like this, I'm going to make you sign a contract for regular sex."

"A contract for regular sex?" she said. "I wasn't aware that this was a business transaction." Angela had never spoken to a man like that in her life.

But it was such a dirty joke, like a *Playboy* cartoon she saw at a friend's house when she was a kid: grey-haired, moustachioed businessman in a fancy lounge bar with a vacuous, big-breasted blonde. He says, "If you don't start feeling those drinks pretty soon, Miss Jones, I'm going to have to ask for separate checks." For years afterwards, Angela thought that *separate checks* was a dirty word.

About two weeks after the funeral, Greg asked her if she'd like to choose one of his cousin's paintings as a keepsake; she asked for the blue T-shirt. This particular evening turned out to be the last time they were naked together; it was also the first time he ever said, "I think we could try it now." *Try*: there's a dirty word. After an hour of humiliation and bland reassurances, Angela walked out of the gingerbread house with the T-shirt painting tucked under her arm and the taste of shame in her mouth.

But there was no going back to dutiful relations once a month either, so a week after she ended it with Greg, Angela left her husband, too. She sat across the kitchen table from him and said, "Nigel, something has happened, I can't explain it, everything has changed." In that one hour, he roared with more passion than she'd seen in fifteen years of marriage. For some reason, she didn't tell him that her lover was gone. Maybe she wanted to make it as easy as she could for Nigel, to let him be jealous of another man instead of something abstract — a hope, an idea.

She didn't tell Greg either, didn't tell him that Nigel threw her out, told her to pack her bags then and there. That Nigel got joint custody, minimum child support, and no maintenance. Angela sometimes takes night shifts at the hospital when the kids are with their dad, just to help pay the bills. She lives in a two-bedroom townhouse in a new subdivision; it reeks of cheap particleboard and plastic. She has asked the agency to always place her with terminal cases — not necessarily AIDS people like the artist either: old people, cancers, even children. She wants to see them through, and their families. Angela likes being there in the place where the darkness meets the light.

She doesn't go out very much, but, a few weeks back, a friend from work took her out on the town, to one of those nightclubs, all flashing lights and pounding music, sweaty men who've had too much to drink, and teenage girls in leather miniskirts and halter tops. It was dreadful, dirty. She couldn't escape from that noise and smoke soon enough, and she'd never go back to a place like that. Angela figures that if the universe sees fit to grant her another boon, it knows where to find her. Sometimes, though, she sets the painting of the blue T-shirt on the mantel, lights a candle on either side, and just enters that place, offering herself in abject humility to a desire that asks for nothing but its own right to exist. When she was a child, her father made the family kneel and pray on the front-room floor, asking forgiveness for fleshly sins Angela couldn't even pronounce, much less envision. Now she kneels before an altar of her own devising, praying for one more chance to know the simple truth of desire before she dies.

*PASSUS SIX*

INNOCENT
April 1997

The buzz in the department lounge is that Stella broke down in class the other day. Clare refuses to believe it, not Stella, not the woman who supervised her first teaching assignment, not the estimable Dr. Morrison, this skinny little spitball of a woman. Not Clare's hero, the first prof she ever had who took her seriously ...

Clare doesn't pee in the shower any more, but she used to. *Ray, standing there at the bathroom sink, scraping the stubble off his face, "I know you pissed in the shower, do you hear me, Clare?" Ray sitting on the can, spitting into a wad of toilet paper* — it was a strange kind of intimacy they had: the sex was lousy always, but they knew each other in a way she's never known anyone, were at ease with each other's bodies, familiar with each other's smells and secrets—

Clare had never peed in the shower before. Not until he accused her of it.

When Clare went back to grad school a few years ago, Stella

bowled her over. Stella had read *everything*. Clare always imag-
ined Stella's dinner parties: soft music playing, exquisite food
— and the conversation. Everyone at the table knew *everything*.
In class, Stella's energy, the stuff she knew. Her confidence, her
authority. She *sang* the Emily Dickinson poems; she said stuff
like, "Of course Darwin's *Origin of Species* appeared in 1859,
and you must consider the impact of that text on the society
Dickens describes." When she taught "The Sick Rose," she did
this wonderful *shtick* about all the possible metaphorical implications of roses and worms, and the students were all laughing
and blushing and so pleased with themselves, so engaged.

But now someone in the coffee room said she'd been teaching "Wife of Bath" in an honours seminar and when she came
to the line that goes:

> *Whan I was yonge and ful of ragerye*
> *Stibbourne and stronge and jolye as a pye,*

she just broke down, stammered, and sunk her head into her
hands. "Dashed out of the room sobbing," they said, "left the
students sitting there with their faces hanging out."

There must be some mistake. Clare remembers how, in the
second week of classes, Stella took her aside one day, whispered,
"There's something we need to discuss. Can we meet in my
office?" Clare trudged down the corridor, her heart sinking —
What had she done wrong? But Stella waved her into a chair
and said, "We need to talk about Ben. How we're going to teach
him. You know the one I mean?"

"Yes," Clare said.

"Well, I found out today, he told me, he's from a small
town up north, went to a Christian school and then two years
of Bible College." In that instant, Clare understood that she
was here as Stella's partner, her colleague, her equal. Clare tried
to focus on the problem of Ben, how to teach this young man,

the textbook of the rose

get him through in one piece. But all the while she couldn't keep the joy from bubbling up. Colleague, peer, equal. Teacher. This startling inclusion.

Stella was saying, "He'll never make it, he's an innocent—" Clare remembers that moment to this day, and she remembers the student, Ben, a tall, blond, tidy young man to whom only Imperialist adjectives seemed to apply. His walking shorts were *crisp*, his manner *jaunty*, his questions and comments in class always *chipper*. Clare was always surprised when he said "Goodbye" instead of "Cheerio." An innocent in a post-Saussurean world.

Clare learned her own innocence in a different kind of school. A marriage like her first can't be easily explained, it's not a made-for-TV movie; everything is so much more complicated. Below the surface there are hidden coercions and participations, there are invitations and complicities. Case in point: Clare's twenty-fourth birthday. No kids yet; the two of them in a basement suite. Ray comes home, late but not too late. And she recognizes the state he is in before she even sees him: she has learned to tell from the weight of his tread on the stairs that, when he stands before her, his body will be inhabited by a wildness; she can almost hear the nerve endings crackle before she sees how everything is clenched inside him, before she sees those white lines around his eyes. And she knows it's going to be bad, but she says, "Hi. How was your day?"

"Not bad."

"Oh. That's good."

He brushes past her and walks down the hall. Now he will spend up to twenty minutes on the can, spitting furtively into a wad of toilet paper (he has piles), then he'll lie in bed and read the paper, and the clock will tick closer to the time of the dinner reservation that he told her to make, but she will wait quietly in the kitchen, she will wait for the signal, whether they are going or not. If they are, she will not know until they get there whether he will speak to her at all during dinner. It's early days yet, and she still hasn't learned to always bring a book.

But it's different today, this day of her twenty-fourth birthday, because he stops suddenly on his way down the hall and he says, "Hey, Babe. I forgot a package in the truck. Go grab it for me, will ya?"

And Clare scurries. She scuttles, like those claws along the floors of stony seas in "Prufrock." It's not that Clare is a stupid person. So why? She can see herself scuttling now, like a near-death experience, looking down on this memory of herself, but then, no. She scuttled, she scurried, out to the truck. It was getting dark, the interior was obscure and, dear God, there were LOTS of things there — coffee cups, a stack of files, his order book. What did he say again, what were his exact words? Dear God, parcel, package, box? There's a box on the floor, full of machine parts, there's this plastic bag, it's got a package inside and the package is shaped like a box. Try. This one.

So she carries the plastic BAG containing a PARCEL or PACK-AGE which appears to contain a BOX into the house. She knows she's probably done it wrong and she's ready — but he looks up from his paper with a genial smile that chills her right through, pats the bed beside him and says, "Happy birthday, Baby. Open it."

*Baby, that's another one. Baby. Clare has always hated those babybaby pop songs, and when she's in the throes of lust, many different words occur to her, some devotional, some obscene — but never "baby." So every time he called her "baby," she'd say, "Don't call me that." You see, she had the general idea. He'd say, "Hey, Baby" and she'd say, "Don't call me baby" and he'd say "Okay, Baby" and laugh, and they did this several hundred times. So she started calling him "baby" and after a while that's all they ever called each*

*other, practically. Hell, she called him "baby" in front of his new*
*wife, it was just so automatic: boy was her face red.*

So poor old Ben, he bobbed and weaved his way through English 200 *circa* 1993. Poor bugger. He called Clare "Missus Taylor"
and Stella "Doctor Morrison." This despite the fact that both
instructors invited the students to use their first names, which
nearly all of them did. At least the ones who remembered what
their names were, which by Christmas was probably close to
sixty per cent.

Ben did okay in the fall. His term paper was a reading of
Marlowe's *Faustus,* in which Clare was terrified he'd quote the
Bible as a secondary source, but he restrained himself and discussed Hellenic cosmology in the poet's Renaissance revision of
the relation between God and man. Even though she gave him
an A on the paper, he dropped in during office hours to go over
it with her, ever so politely questioning her insistence on gender-
neutral pronouns.

Clare's marriage to Ray ended five years ago. The funny thing
is, it wasn't she who left. The funny thing is that she cried for
days. A month before Ray left, the young intern at Emergency
who set Clare's wrist said, "There are places you can call, you
know. To get help. Think of your children." She didn't call a
shelter though, didn't call anyone, just fell madly in love with
that intern when Ray brushed through the curtains of her cubi-
cle and the two men eyed each other with a raw hatred that
jolted right through her; pure power — they locked eyes, it was
fabulous. Clare could tell the intern was scared, Dr. Mohtad
was his name, but he didn't back down; he turned to her with

elaborate courtesy, like Ben would have, she thinks, and he said, "Are you all right in here?"

"Yes, fine," she said. "It's okay." He wouldn't leave till she agreed to let him go. So she could. Mere power.

Like Stella some days, when she really gets into it; she just hits on some idea and runs with it and a kind of brightness flows from her, Clare can see the students sort of pushed back in their chairs, like in one of those magazine ads for big stereo speakers — this bright passion, this power. That's what Clare has always wanted, she just didn't know it. Or rather, she didn't know how to name it.

*I know you piss in the shower, he says; your mother never taught you the most basic hygiene; you're filthy; you've got footrot; your hair looks like you combed it with a grenade; you send the kids to nursery school with last night's ketchup all over their faces; this house stinks; the carpet stinks—*

But when it came to despising her family, Ray was without peer — Sunday dinner, Mother's Day picnic, the Christmas concert, no one immune: *self-serving asshole, fucking wuss, did you see his outfit; did you hear what she said, stupid bitch.* Now, Ray, don't say that. Ray, don't. Clare's furtive pleasure, that splendid surrender, like masturbating under the covers or bumming a cigarette two years after you've quit — you know you shouldn't be doing it but it just feels so good.

The winter term posed a bit of a problem for Ben. He aced the quizzes and midterm of course, but the essay topics were pretty well twentieth century, and Clare's heart sank when she picked up his paper and saw that he'd decided to do the question of legal versus moral guilt in *Blood Relations*, the play about Lizzie Borden. We're in trouble now, she thought.

But no. He walked the walk. He danced through those mine-fields of nebulous distinctions like someone who'd grown up watching MTV. Clare was pleased at first, then worried. He's lying, he's caved in, this is not right, this is not how he sees the world. It was probably unprofessional, but she called him in, said, "Listen, you don't have to do this——" and he just looked at her with eyes hard as pebbles and his jaunty smile, and said, "Mrs. Taylor, whatever do you mean?" Pleading innocence.

*The scrape of the razor over Ray's cheek, water running, Clare towelling off. "I know you, I know you do it, I know you piss in the shower" and Clare, wide-eyed, alive to the danger but holding it to her anyway — the slave's rebellion is such a paltry thing, to everyone but the slave.*

Ray left and Clare cried for days. He was right about a lot of things. He said he'd find someone else before she did, and he was right about that. After a month or two she called Dr. Mohtad, just to say hello. Called him again a week later. Played it cool at first and he was kind, but she just couldn't stop herself from dialling his number, and after a while he stopped returning her calls and then he stopped answering the phone and then his roommate called her up one night after she'd left about six messages and said, "Look, there's no sense in this." Clare knew he was right, but she was so wired that she just started blubbering, and Larry, the roommate, said, "You probably need to get out of the house for a while. Go for a walk or a run."

"What about my kids?"

"Get a sitter."

"Yeah right, at 11:30 on a Tuesday night? Dream on."

"I'll come over and watch your kids."

"You? I don't know you from a hole in the ground and you think——"

"Look, I just got off work, can't sleep anyhow. I'm a paramedic. You can't qualify if you've got a criminal record. Give me your address and I'll sit with your kids until you walk this off."

Clare walked for three hours and, when she came back, he made her a cup of tea and massaged her feet. No one had ever massaged her feet before. It wasn't till their third date that Larry confessed, "Nobody ever asked me whether I had a criminal record or not. I mean, maybe they checked without asking, but I kinda made that part up."


It's nowhere near as simple as it seems, Clare can't explain it really: *You just begin this relatively whole person, standing on your own two feet, and you're knocked down and you get up and you're knocked down and you get back up and then maybe one time you only get onto your knees before the next blow, and maybe the next time you're just crouching, or sitting, and after a while you sort of don't remember any more what all the way up even looks like.* The twenty-fourth birthday present? Clare sat on the bed, prim in her going-out-to-dinner dress, and opened the PACKAGE. Inside the PACKAGE was a cardboard BOX. Inside the BOX were four glasses with gold rims and a scrolled message on the sides — "May you be in heaven half an hour before the devil knows you're dead." Tucked between the glasses was a beautifully lettered parchment recipe for Irish coffee. Clare doesn't drink Irish coffee. She doesn't drink at all, she never has, it makes her sick. "Thank you, Baby," she said.

But no, it's more complicated than that: The last spring Ray and Clare were together, she was walking down to the corner store on a Sunday afternoon, with Emma. The baby was at home, napping beneath the Sunday paper with his dad. Early April, the air thick with promise, the grass still brown and dry under Emma's red boots as she toddled along the boulevard, singing "All the gumdrops are gumdrops and gumdrops," swinging around on those wooden poles that people use to plug in their cars, they're like upside-down Ls. Then Clare heard this barky old voice and noticed an old man on the porch of his house, a nasty-looking old man in a soiled brown overall unbuttoned over a yellowed undershirt. Clare prepared to trill out some neighbourly greeting, "Lovely day, spring at last," but the old man crooked his finger at Emma and said "C'mere, kid." Emma turned cautiously, approaching the gate. Clare was right behind, her hand on Emma's back, *What does he want, to give her a candy? How will I get it away from her if he does?* and the old man stood there, squinting on his porch, and crouched down to Emma and said, "Kid, if you don't want your ass kicked through your shoulders, keep yer fuckin' hands offa my pole."

He had gone back inside and shut the door before Clare could react. Emma's whole face trembled. "Mama?" was all she could think of to say.

So Clare bought her two sour soothers instead of just the one, and they headed back home on the other side of the street. All the time, each step, Clare was thinking, *Okay, I'll take care of this, I must not, I must never say a word to Ray, he'd freak, Christ only knows what he'll do. So no, I just go up to the door and I say, "Look, this is a three-year-old child here, you shouldn't——"* *No, I'll say, "If you ever speak to my child like that again, I'll——"*

But they have passed the old man's house by now, and besides, she can't go with Emma, the kid's terrified. And she can't tell Emma to stand at the end of the block and wait: What if she runs out into the traffic? No, Clare must take her daughter home first, leave her at home, and then come back and march up to that door and say *Who do you think you are, speaking to my daughter like that? She's a little kid, she made a mistake, she won't do it again, but I think you owe both of us an apology and I'm going to stand here until you make it——* But what does she tell Ray? What if he's asleep? What if he's not asleep and Emma tells him what happened? How does Clare get out of the house again, say she forgot something at the store? What can she say she forgot?——

She told him, of course. She told him the moment she walked through the door. She woke him up to tell him.

It was Larry who talked Clare into going back to grad school. She got the MA a couple of years ago, and they hired her as a sessional with full benefits right after she convocated. They're even giving her maternity leave. The baby's due in June. Clare ran into Ben in the hallway recently, a week or two before that weird story about Stella began making the rounds. Ben bobbed and smiled and said, "Hello, Mrs. Taylor, or should I say Professor Taylor now?" He's completing an honours BA in Religious Studies. He said, "You know, Professor Taylor, you have managed to convince me that certain aspects of contemporary literary theory are not entirely without merit." Clare smiled into the glint of mischief in his cool blue eyes and said, "I'm glad to hear it, Ben." She was thinking that maybe William

Blake had it right: we begin in innocence, acquire experience, and ultimately aspire to a state of organized innocence. Maybe that's it. At least she doesn't pee in the shower any more. That's got to count for something.

*Ray wasn't much of a talker, so she never really found out what happened. All Ray said was that, when he went to the door, the guy's wife answered and said her husband was out back, in the garage. So that's all she has to go on, but it's enough. She can smell the musty old garage with oil rags stuffed in cans, old paintbrushes rotting with damp in murky pickle jars. There's a forty-watt bulb in the rafters, and a layer of grease and dust on everything. She can smell the fear on the old geezer; see the sweat blossom on his forehead, around his mouth. He starts to speak, but Ray simply gathers that brown shirt in his fist, the air just crackles, and in seconds the old guy's on his knees, water gathering in his eyes, his lungs heaving. He's so scared he pisses himself. Clare can picture it plain as day, Ray stepping out into the alley and delicately wiping his hands, and the old guy lying there on the floor of his garage in a puddle of discount motor oil and his own piss, blinking back tears———*

Clare pictures that scene from time to time, conjures it up, despite foot massages, despite safety. Now and then that picture floats into her mind, and at last she can name the darkness that she enters as her own.

*CHANSON D'AVENTURE*

THE TEXTBOOK OF THE ROSE
August 1997

RETREAT/NO EXIT looms dayglo orange out of the prairie night, but Stella speaks paradox fluently, with a minor in oxymoron, and she slows her car just in time to make the turnoff.

A banner draped above the front doors proclaims "Colloquium 97 — Welcome." The foyer of St. Jerome's is a high-ceilinged room, the stone fireplace in the centre casting warm shadows on grouped figures, the air filled with a congenial hum of voices and laughter. Someone calls out her name, and then Diana's hug engulfs her in the scent of woodsmoke and Dove soap. "Bill and the kids are camping at Cypress Hills. They're picking me up next weekend."

Stella glances at the crowd. "Dear God, I hope there's no one I know."

"Well, there's me."

"Yeah, but I mean someone who might report me to the thought police."

"Trust me. You'll like it here. We've put you down for a talk on Monday night, okay? By 'talk' I mean one page of notes. Not a paper."

"Fine. Point me to the bar."

The subtitle for this gathering is "keeping the conversation going." Diana talked her into it: "Revel in the open-endedness of it, Stella. Imagine nobody expecting you to know anything for sure. A break from the place of pinch and crab. Open questions."

Stella likes the sound of that.

*The first time she made love to him she mapped the flaccid breasts, drained of their flesh by suckling mouths, the jagged scar from navel to groin, souvenir of a doctor who had no time for bikini lines, and besides, women over thirty look better in a one-piece anyway. The post-partum souvenir of haemorrhoids she saves for the end of the tour.*

Next morning, at breakfast, she carries her tray over to Diana's table. "Stella, I'd like you to meet my friend Nigel. He's in Religious Studies at the host university. And these are his students Michelle and Stephen." Stella shakes hands with a lanky man whose smile appears to cause him pain, and nods hello to the students, an ethereal girl in India print and a hulking young man dressed in black.

Diana says, "It was Nigel who got me the interview at the vocational college. He knows the head of the New Canadians program. I was feeling like such a failure. Defrocked. Shunned. But I've just finished summer session and discovered that I love teaching ESL. The students are so motivated, so eager to learn. And for the first time in years, I feel like what I'm teaching is worthwhile. All those years in the department, I told myself that it mattered, that not knowing *King Lear* and *Tess of the D'Urbervilles* was to live the unexamined life. But, in all the political turmoil, even that got lost, and by the time I left, I'd be standing in the classroom, trying to preach the new gospel, and all the time thinking: How can I say this, do I have the authority, do I have the right? Grammar is refreshingly straight-forward——"

"You're lucky," Stella says. "What I wouldn't give for a little motivation and gratitude. Swear to God, if I ever have one more grad student furrow his or her brow and say, 'I'm not sure whether those two notions occupy the same space,' I cannot be held responsible. And the undergrads, dear God. They quote *TV Guide* as a secondary source. They cite Oprah. All these sullen boys at the back of the room, ball caps pulled low on their foreheads, these big meaty arms folded across their chests. You can see them staring you down, defying you: *Just try and make this interesting, you old bitch, just go ahead and fucking try.* And the girls with symmetrical salon curls bursting out of the backs of *their* ball caps, which are just like the boys' only cleaner and more expensive. And every one of them a walking adver-tisement — Spirit River, Bum Equipment, Northern Lights, Gap, Nike, Esprit, Coors Light, Blue Jays, Bust Loose. I feel like I'm on a friggin' bus!"

Stella suddenly remembers that her table companions in-clude two students. "Oops. Present company excepted, of course." The girl smiles unhappily and twirls a lock of unpermed blonde hair, but the boy smiles warmly. His eyes are beautiful, sea green flecked with gold. He says, with a laugh in his voice, "No, please. Go on. I enjoy hearing you talk." The word *enjoy* rolls out of his mouth like a ripe plum.

Nigel says, "Well, there's a lot of that going around, but out here the strain doesn't seem quite so virulent, somehow. Diana tells me you're from the prairies originally."

"Yes, I was born in a little village about thirty miles from here. But we moved to the coast when I was nine."

"Do you have a sense of homecoming, here, now?" The young man asks old questions. What does *homecoming* mean, Stella wonders.

"You know what would really make me feel at home? Visiting the lake I swam in as a child. Willow Lake, it's just south of here. I remember the smell of sage and that kind of swampy green colour of the water, the warmth of it. The gravelly beach littered with freshwater clamshells. Mountain lakes always seem disgustingly cold and pristine and kind of, I don't know, unwelcoming. Too perfect, too self-consciously scenic."

"Willow Lake?" says Stephen. "My parents have a cottage there. I could give them a call, and you could go for your swim at their place——"

God, he's adorable, Stella thinks. He can't be in grad school yet or he'd know that you never ever admit to a cottage.

*That first time, she mapped the maternal souvenirs — the crooked, once-broken finger, smashed as she lunged to catch a falling TV set that Zak had just pulled off the shelf after uttering his first sentence: "B'oon gone!"*

She drives back to Cottonwood, one day. The village church is a ruin, abandoned, the arched windows boarded up, crows cawing from the weathered steeple. On a board nailed over a broken window, someone has scrawled in white paint:

> I am just an emty
> shell inside
> please don't hurt
> me any more

The August heat stuns her, the earth hums with life. She strolls through the graveyard where she played as a child, the familiar Scots and Ukrainian names, those fallen in the flu epidemic of

1918, infant graves from the thirties. Her grandfather's post office and general store, which stood at the crossroads, is now gone. Obliterated, even the foundation filled in. Her parents, retired in their Qualicum Beach trailer park, have told her this, but it's still a shock to see it firsthand. A farmer has planted acres of sunflowers there. Stella leans out the window of her car as she is leaving and takes a picture, a field of yellow stretching to the horizon, the top half of the frame a mild blue.

*She maps her body for him, the enlarged and misshapen toe, rammed into Miranda as Stella stepped over her with a basket of laundry. (An injury which would signify differently if Miranda had been huddled over a Science Fair project instead of watching* Sabrina, the Teenage Witch, *and Stella merely absorbed in a phone conversation.)*

Within a few days, Stella falls into a routine: an early-morning walk in the hills; then breakfast, usually with Diana, Nigel, and his students. The rest of the morning is spent reading, stretching on a patch of grass outside her dorm, sitting in an armchair in the lounge and watching the horizon shimmer in the heat. After lunch, Stella attends a lecture or seminar or poetry reading from the list of the day's activities. After supper, a stroll in the hills or a walk into town for a drink with Nigel and Diana. At first, Stella merely notes that she's feeling a bit "odd;" it takes a few days for more explicit adjectives like "peaceful" and "calm" to present themselves as descriptors of this unfamiliar state of mind.

Stella has always loved the familiar pattern of the Welsh tales, the French romances. The confiding voice of the narrator

— he'll get you there despite the digressions — just relax and enjoy the journey. Her favourite image, though, is the crow eating blood off the snow. Sometimes a falcon kills a duck, or a hawk a pigeon — but she likes the crow, his glossy black feathers, his triumphant caw, the glistening blood on the sparkling snow. Any dictionary of symbolism can give you the basic picture — white for purity, red for lust, black for death. Desire stains us, makes us mortal. The red, white, and black of the scene always reminds the questing hero of his beloved: her jet black hair, her pure white skin, red red lips, and rosy cheeks — think of Blancheflor, Snow White, even Gawain's loathly lady turns red, white, and black to make the happy ending:

> Sweet blushes stayned her rud-red cheek,
> Her eyes were black as sloe,
> The ripening cherry swelled her lippe,
> And all her neck was snow.

Love and desire, red blood on white snow, a black crow to feast on what remains.

Stella's talk is on the Regeneration Motif in the Arthurian Tales. She knows how to gauge her audience, and tonight she pitches it a bit low-brow — lots of undergrads and civilians in the crowd, so she punches it up with a lot of sexual innuendo, without neglecting judicious mention of the current critics, just to make sure the academics take her seriously. The loathly lady, the Wife of Bath as the proto-feminist; two men vying for the same woman; regeneration through romantic quest; the grail a witches' cauldron, a womb. She suggests that the Grail Quest is a vestige of the prepatriarchal goddess religions so viciously scourged from Europe in the Middle Ages, and her concluding salvo is met with vigorous applause as well as a serendipitous clap of thunder from the storm that has been threatening all day. Just as the applause dies, the lights abruptly go out, and the retreatants move into the lounge to drink wine and watch several types of lightning dance through the night sky.

Stella has trouble settling down to sleep that night, and after a time she arises from her rumpled single bed and peeks out into the corridor. Silence. She stuffs her nightdress into a pair of baggy shorts and throws on a cardigan as she pads quietly down the hall. The storm has increased in magnificence; wind howls at the doors, and rain slashes in diagonal sheets at the glass, so Stella opts for the smoking parlour, a dismal little room with a rattling air cleanser, drab furniture, and amateur oil paintings. He's in there, that young man. Stephen. It is an awkward moment: he is shirtless, she unusually rumpled and bulging — but they both smile and settle in. "What are you doing in here, Stephen? You don't even smoke." He smiles. "I'm casting about for a suitable vice. Can I bum one of those?" They smoke in companionable silence. Stella is conscious of his eyes on her tanned chest, warm brown against a ruff of white cotton lace. She has never, until this moment, considered her left collarbone erogenous, or even attractive, but she is surprised to find herself suspecting that it might be both.

She keeps her own gaze fixed on a particularly bad still life just above his left shoulder. Nigel has told her that Stephen, an honours undergrad in Religious Studies, normally spends his summers as a retreatant at a Franciscan abbey up north. For five hours each day, Stephen hoes potatoes or picks saskatoons, in exchange for room and board. As she stubs out her cigarette, Stella says, "May I ask why you're investigating vice?"

"Hmm. Not sure. Perhaps I'm finding, lately, that virtue is its own punishment."

Stella realigns her misbuttoned cardigan and rises to leave. "I've certainly found that to be the case, but, unlike you, I did not choose virtue but had it thrust upon me. Goodnight, Stephen," she says.

Earlier in the day, Stella had sat in an armchair in the lounge, going over her notes one last time, gazing out the windows overlooking the valley. Out on the lawn there were pockets of retreatants talking together, a few solitary figures engrossed in their books or meditations or sunbathing. And Stephen, moving. A figure in black, gracefully moving in what seemed like slow motion. Even at a distance he looked huge. His face was set in concentration as he moved his body through a series of familiar stretches — sun salutation, hero's pose, warrior, mountain, tree. Stella smirked to herself and glanced around to see who he might be performing for. That patchouli-scented trance-poet? The buxom Englishwoman from Memorial? All the same, she thinks, watching Stephen, whoever he's doing it for, he's lovely. It only takes a split second for this pleasure to dissolve into what is now all too familiar to Stella; it's what she can only describe as a "pang" and it happens, these days, at any hint of sexual happiness — a grad student's lapel button that asks "Have you had your orgasm today?", an elderly couple strolling hand in hand, an offhand remark from a friend like "He's a sensitive lover" or "The sex is great." Even words and phrases like "seeing," "dating," "going out with." This pang hurts Stella. It reminds her of her exile, her exemption from a world of effortless intimacy. It makes tears rim her eyes. It weighs down the stone in her chest.

*She maps the arthritic joints from various accidents of domesticity: a thumb turned backwards as it caught a child falling from his bike, an index finger smashed against a suddenly-rearing blonde head, a slashed toe unfortunately placed beneath the blade of a freshly sharpened hockey skate. A scarred knee from a drunken and tearful encounter with a coffee table at 3:00 A.M. And the line, she calls it the divorce line, a thin white slash, fine and straight and razor-thin, on her brow. People have asked how it happened, an accident? ("Sort of — my marriage," Stella sometimes says), but the really strange thing is that it just appeared there one morning. It just appeared there. The morning after Jake finally spit it out, finally told her everything.*

"The pose of the child."

"Huh? Oh, hi, Stephen. You startled me."

"Sorry. That's a nice posture."

"One of my personal favourites."

Stella is uncertain whether to continue her sun salutation or just sit up and talk with him. He's standing against the sun and all she can see is his silhouette — looming, a solid black wall of male flesh, muscle, and bone. She knows that it's a breach of practice to stop halfway through, but for him to speak to her was equally impolite. She decides to finish the movement — back down to pose of the child, a slow careful slide into little cobra, relax the shoulders, keep the legs and pelvis active, stretch the spine out and slightly up, then swing back into downward dog. Her eyes are closed, but she can sense him moving toward her feet. Is he checking out her ass? *Fuck him*, Stella thinks. Downward dog, her body forming a perfect inverted V, breathe, straight elbows, inch the heels down, hold. Then, swing the right leg through; left leg joins; drooping down like a wilted flower; releasing the shoulders, the neck; feeling the hamstrings stretch and release; bend the knees, swing up from the hips; hands over the head; namaste; mountain pose.

"Lovely," he says.

"Am I supposed to thank you? I've never considered Hatha yoga a competitive sport."

"I mean, it's nice to watch. You look like it pleases you."

"Oh. Well, yes. It does." *Pleases.* She likes the way he says that word. He seems disinclined to speak again, is smiling and looking at the distant hills. Stella looks too. Rolling gentle hills, the dusky green colour of sage, though up close still surprisingly green. The faraway hum of traffic on Highway 4. The meadow below the retreat, grazing cattle. The sky a subdued blue today, softened by voluptuous clouds floating on the edges of the horizon, like a ruff. "The clouds are up so high here." Stella is alarmed to realize that she has said this aloud.

His response is equally dreamy: "I've been looking at the big hill over there, across the tracks, but before the highway — do you see the one I mean?"

"Yes, I love the look of it, the shape. It's like Gorsedd Arberth."

"What's that?"

"The hill of wonders, from the *Mabinogion*, the Welsh tales."

"Hill of wonders."

"Someone says to Pryderi, 'Lord, it is the property of this hill that whenever a man of royal blood sits on it, one of two things happens: he receives blows and wounds, or else he sees a wonder.'"

He laughs. "Amazing. The hill of wonders. Would you like to walk over there with me after supper?"

*The razor scar, the divorce line, is the second-last stop on the tour. The haemorrhoids provide the finale, her glorious maternal souvenir, a relief map of the Rockies protruding from her behind. He likens it to a rosette. Stella tells him how, if she ever wrote her autobiography, she'd simply describe all these scarred and damaged places on her body, and tell the story of each one. And the tale would end with these words: So Stella got up in the morning, had a good cry, stuffed her asshole back inside her body and carried on with her day.*

To describe Stella's life, you need only to know this: Last September, she was required, twice within one day, to respond to a query on a form sent home from her children's school. Stella has a couple of graduate degrees, she's no fool, but the question absolutely stumped her. It read: "What sorts of activities do you and your family enjoy together in your leisure time?"

Stella could not answer this question. She sat, sucking her pen, wondering "Does eating meals together count, on the rare nights of no hockey, skating, or Guides, runs to Children's Emergency or night classes? What *do* we do with our time, after work and school? Well, let's see. I nag them to do their homework, unload the dishwasher, and clean up their rooms. I do laundry, and fold it on the dining-room table while they watch TV or play computer games. Then it's time to hound them into bath and bed while I pick up all the junk off the floor."

Sometimes, the notion of a board game flits across the screen of Stella's brain — a fire, cups of convivial hot chocolate — but by the time supper is served and cleaned up, fights refereed, school work and books gathered, one chapter of a story read aloud, teeth brushed, a call from a friend taken, pyjamas donned, a dispute over comic books settled, it's 9:15 and time for bed. The snuggles and glasses of water and "Mom can I ask you something?" go on till 10:00 or 10:30. Then Stella marks papers, pays bills, or preps a novel for class tomorrow till midnight or so, and the day ends. What sorts of activities do Stella and her family enjoy during their leisure hours?

"Basic Survival" is what Stella writes on the forms.

*Stella explores his body. Acres of smooth light brown flesh, absolutely unscarred. Even his body hair is silky. She perches on his generous behind and feels like she's sitting on the hill of wonders.*

Stella scoops a ring of milk froth from the rim of her cup and pops the spoon into her mouth. She and Nigel have driven to Nan's Nook, the only purveyor of cappuccino in a radius of thirty miles. "Would you like another?" Nigel asks.

"No, thanks, I've achieved perfect caffeine toxicity. So you've been on your own how long?"

"Six months. I'm still in shock, I'm afraid. I thought we had an understanding, Angie was always such a sweet person. She became a stranger that night, I don't know how I didn't see it coming——"

"Seeing it coming doesn't help anyhow, you still get hit by the train. With us, it started after our son was born. Jake sidled up to me one night when I'd finally gotten the baby down and said 'When are you coming back?'"

"To him, you mean?"

"Yeah, guess so. I don't even remember what I said, I just felt this wave of irritation, revulsion even. As if he was just one more person wanting a piece of me. And then a couple of years later, we took a holiday, rented a little cabin in the mountains — Miranda was a baby and Zak was about three. One afternoon, I'd gotten the baby down and wanted to get Zak out of the house, so I said to Jake, 'We're just going down to the playground. Can you watch Miranda?' Sure, he said, not looking up from his book. So there I am, about half a mile from the cabin, pushing Zak on the swing and trying to keep the mosquitoes off us both.... And out of the corner of my eye I see a shape, a familiar blur, moving on the road. I look over and it's Jake."

"He left her?"

"He went out for a run. A run! I'll tell you, I spent the worst ten minutes of my life stumbling back down that pathway through the forest. I'm slick with sweat, Zak's yelling 'More park, more park!' Nothing in the world is heavier than a hot, pissed-off three-year-old, right? ... She was fine, of course. Fast asleep. But that afternoon, I knew what Jake was telling me. Despite the protests, the rationalizations, the 'I thought you meant' or 'I didn't hear what you said.' No, what he meant was: 'You're on your own.'"

Stella has been single long enough not to be surprised by this easy exchange of confidences between the maritally battered. Nigel, however, seems still to be finding his way. "Ready?" he says, flushing slightly. "We'll just have time for me to show you this little valley I found."

She watches Nigel's hands sliding a cassette into the tape deck and tries to imagine those hands on her body, but she can't. Has she even gotten close to telling him the truth of her marriage? What about those second-trimester nights, Stella alone in their room, while Jake watched hockey in the den, letting her "get her rest." Stella, in their bed, wrenched with near-hallucinatory fantasies that leave her dripping from every orifice, mind and body surrendered utterly, scarily, to a porno serial that would make "O" blush. This strange place she visited night after night seemed too personal to share with him. She couldn't let Jake appropriate this pleasure, claim it for himself ... no, this was hers alone. He would only have gotten in the way.

She won't tell Nigel any of this, of course. Besides, Stella knows, without knowing how, that sexual fulfilment eluded

Nigel in his marriage, a fact that makes his wife's sudden defection sting all the more. She also knows, though he has not said so, that Nigel has taken a Suddenly Single class or perhaps a Personal Development seminar, and that he is seeing a counsellor regularly, one who is working with him on forgiving his father, on redefining himself as a man. He probably hasn't done any naked drumming, but he's read Robert Bly.

Stella knows these things because that's what the men in *her* Surviving Divorce group were like. She's been there, done that — Diana talked her into it after the last meltdown. Oh yes, Stella has known them all, all those humiliations of the seduced and betrayed. The affirmations, the lists of Twenty Things I Like About Myself. The abject desperation of the telepersonals, dutiful dates, Singles Functions, Post-it notes on the bathroom mirror: You are beautiful. You are smart. You are lovable.

In any case, Nigel is a man she already knows, quite well. She knows all the conversations they will have. Earnest conversations, the hesitations and risks, the confessions ... the misunderstandings, the lengthy negotiations, "What you said and what I meant." Their relationship, if they choose to have one, will not be fallen into but forged. Stella knows these things already, knows them all as she sits beside this kind man, listening to Miles Davis on the car stereo, driving through the blinding brightness of the prairie afternoon.

People their age, Stella's and Nigel's, all talk the talk in their personal growth groups, and at gatherings at the bar after work on Friday nights: the hard work of relationship, the compromise, the give and take, true adulthood at last. But every damn one of them longs for *coup de foudre, la folie* — why are all the words for it in French, Stella wonders. Is English too dull a language to even accommodate such notions? No, no, there it is, right there in Gawain — "joye out of mynde."

*Dame Ragnell says to Gawain, "If you marry me, I will tell you the most important secret in the world. I will tell you what women want."*

The dirt road appears dry on the surface, and is dry on the level, but the moment they crest the hill and begin to descend, mud oozes up from beneath the veneer of dust. By the time they reach the bottom, Nigel's Saab is sliding helplessly, its tires inches deep in muck. There is no point in trying to drive anywhere, backwards or forwards. Last night's storm, of course. They'd both forgotten about it. They will have to walk. Nigel eases the car to the side of the road, and they both get out. Stella laughs as they trudge up the slope, mud sucking at their sneakers. The road edge works best, they can get a bit of purchase on the weeds and must stop frequently to scrape their shoes with a stick.

Stella and Nigel emerge from the valley and find themselves in an ocean of wheatfields, stretching before them and on either side. The sun blazes, yesterday's storm clouds doze on the horizon, the clouds here pile up so high. Stella has brought her Walkman. She starts up her Pavarotti tape and insists that Nigel and she take turns listening. When it is her turn, she skips and smiles, stretches and waves her arms, conducting the wheatfields and soaring voice, and revelling in the endless possibilities of walking down this road with this man. Pure freedom. Passing the headphones to Nigel ensures that he will not talk, that he will not apologize any more; that he will not fuss, at least no more than he already has: "You must think I'm such a fool. I should've known the road would be like that. We'll miss dinner and you'll be late for your meeting with Stephen——" She has told him about this change in their habitual schedule. That's why they met for coffee instead of after-dinner drinks. Stella believes that she has nothing to hide.

The tape runs out after forty-five minutes, and they're still a mile or so from the retreat. Stella takes pity on Nigel, returns the Walkman to her bag, decides to let him say whatever it is he wants to say.

Apologies first. An offer to drive to town and buy her a sandwich. Of course he'll have to borrow her car. Anything in particular she likes? Tuna? On brown or white? An apple, some chips, what flavour? Something to drink?

Confession next. He feels like he's made a mess out of his life, sometimes he doesn't know where to turn or what to do next. Keeping strong for the sake of his kids is all that keeps him going.

And a declaration. "Stella, I'm so attracted to you——" Even though Stella was expecting something like this, it still comes to her as a surprise and a delight. The last few days have cleared her somehow. The stone is barely there, she's free of rehearsals, anticipations, fears, regrets. She is simply ready to welcome what comes. She can't remember the last time the notion that *anything could happen now* aroused in her something other than dread.

His embrace is stiff with terror, and Stella is relieved to pull away, to resume walking, to still his outpourings with the approach of a group of retreatants taking an after-dinner stroll. Stella waves. Nigel tries a smile.

Stephen is not in the lounge. She finds his name in the directory and checks his room. It's down in the students' wing, right at the end of the hall. Near a fire exit. But he's not there. The front lawn, no. No note on her door. She decides that he must have headed out on his own. Perhaps she'll meet him on the pathway, or maybe he's already up on the hill. She's half an hour late, after all. Perhaps he's angry, or perhaps not. She strides out, gets just a few yards down the path when she remembers that she hasn't checked the Smoking Parlour, and she turns back.

He's there. He's sitting in the Smoking Parlour, talking with the most elderly member of the group, a grizzle-voiced retired teacher who tells everyone who will listen about the recent death of his wife.

Stephen smiles when he sees Stella. "There you are," he says. "Are you ready to go?"

The pathway winds between the hills, and Stephen and Stella walk easily together, talk easily. About yoga, about types of meditation, about Stephen's progression through these disciplines to t'ai chi and then martial arts, about Stella's research on medieval concepts of gender and divinity, about Stephen's honours project on Sufi and Transcendentalism. But what pleases Stella even more are the meditative pauses, the companionable silences, as when they both stop to watch a solitary crow on a dead branch, scolding and cawing. On every first date in recent years, Stella has been subjected to a frenetic rush of breathless talk, as if her companion is auditioning, and must not forget to show her every valuable hockey card in his collection. This torrent of verbiage, this anxious performance, usually so exhausts and depresses Stella that second dates are rare.

Not that this is a date or anything.

The crow scolds them both severely, then takes flight, the rush of air against his wings audible in the silence of the August evening. Stephen and Stella walk on, leaving the path, clambering through waist-high grass and then over a barbed-wire fence. Stephen is solicitous — "Careful, are you through?" — offering his hand, and then they follow the railway tracks. Stella tries to walk the metal band, but totters off after only a few steps. Stephen stays on longer. He is a large man, over six feet tall and very solid and strong — but exquisitely graceful.

Dense bush separates them from the hill they're trying to reach; they decide to walk on past it to a place where the bush seems to thin out, then cut back along a cowpath that traverses the ridge.

Pure pleasure, in his company. Stella has never met anyone like him. He is thoughtful, serious, kind. He doesn't own a television, doesn't drive a car or ride a bike. He says, "I'm very conscious of not doing anything that might hurt my body."

"But then you walk into a kick-boxing ring."

"Ninjutsu, actually. Well, yes. I know it seems a paradox, but really, for me, these matches are a kind of meditation, too. A sort of loving-kindness meditation, in some weird sense."

Stella says, "Hey I did that one once at the end of my yoga class. I had no problem with it at first. You picture people you love, your family — fine, I picture my kids: 'May you be filled with loving kindness.' Next you think of friends: 'May you be well' — no problem. Then on to strangers — the checkout person at Safeway, my students: 'May you be peaceful and at ease.' I'm thinking: hey, I'm a natural at this. But then my teacher says, 'Now picture someone who has made you suffer': BOOM, there's my ex-husband, and I struggle and stiffen up and my whole body goes tense with the effort and I'm thinking: *May your cock not fall off, I mean it, really——*"

Stephen laughs, says, "I remember the day I got through that part. It was a real achievement." Stella longs to ask who, but she doesn't. She can see no harm in this man; he is utterly without guile. He says, "Lately, I've been trying to work with the idea that those who make us suffer are the most powerful teachers."

Stella turns this idea over. What did she learn from Jake? That men are scum, that no one can be trusted, that she's a fool. That after seventeen years she was nothing to him, merely an object standing in his way. Then a memory comes — she's

lying on a rumpled single bed in her dorm at the university.
The bed is against the wall beside a window with the curtains
drawn, cheap polyester curtains, avocado green, that don't close
all the way, leaving a narrow shaft of morning sunlight slashing
through the centre of the room. *The Allman Brothers Live at the
Fillmore East* is turned low on the stereo, "Whipping Post."
Jake snores and stirs beside her as Stella reaches over him to
light a smoke. She tells Stephen, "So you blow the smoke in a
smooth straight line across the room, and then it hits that wall
of sunlight and splat! As if it was hitting a brick wall, the smoke
literally bounces, disperses, spreads, sort of smooshes flat and
swirly. I remember lying there just watching this, fascinated,
and then Jake woke up. I said, 'Look at this, isn't it incredible?'
And he said, 'The sunlight heats the air and makes the mol-
ecules move faster so the smoke can't pass through.'"

"And was that something you wanted to know?"

"No, I guess not. I was pissed off at him, and then mad at
myself for getting pissed off over nothing."

"Breaking an enchantment is not nothing."

"Yeah, you're right. That's what he did. Do you think we
should start heading up the hill now? The bush looks a little
thinner here."

When they leave the tracks, the going gets tough.

The night Stella met Jake, at a Grateful Dead concert at the
Pacific Coliseum, she was wired on acid and Jake had been
smoking opium. The acid made Stella awestruck, humble and
quiet, while the opium smoothed out Jake's angry rawness. They
sold each other a bill of pharmaceutically enhanced goods, and
then had to live with the results for a couple of decades. Once
in a while, she seriously considers sending Charlotte a thank-
you note.

From the sunny openness of the tracks, voluptuous hills on all sides, a blue sky fringed with soft clouds, they are suddenly enclosed. Low shrubs, bushes, tortuous patches of head-high Canada thistle with hairy purple crowns. Trees, storm-damaged or dead, toppled over in their path. Dry bare branches that snap and poke, leaf-laden ones that spring and slap. The air alive with an insect hum, a steady drone. Not a stir of breeze, just dense, buzzing, leaden heat. And the smells. Rot and manure and muck. They're on a cowpath that leads to a slough. A wide smelly slough ringed with trampled mud.

They retrace their steps, follow another path. Again, they come to a muddy edge. No access. They laugh. "This is turning out to be an adventure," Stephen says. Stella listens for a trace of apology and hears none. "In the Welsh tales," she says, "ritual delay is intrinsic to the story. It spins out the tale. And it hardens the hero to his quest." Any other man Stella has ever known would make a joke about this, anything from a mild smirk to a crude remark centring on the concept of "hard." Not Stephen. His hand warm on her shoulder, he says, "We'd best keep going then. What about this way?"

Again and again they try to find their way around the slough. They back up, bushwhack a while, pick up another trail — but each attempt brings them up to the edge of the motionless fetid water. If it were a stream or a river, Stella would suggest wading across. But not this. Motionless opaque beige surface, tufted with patches of livid bluegreen scum, crawling with insect life.

Stella and Jake started at the university in the mid-seventies for the politics, and stayed for the money. They were both so bright,

so ambitious, and so outrageous that they kept receiving fund-
ing, scholarships, grants. When people ask Stella why she became a medievalist, she sometimes says, "Because the texts are
like acid without the side-effects. Like that scene in *Peredur*
where he's questing along and comes to a stream with black
sheep on one side and white ones on the other. And every time
a sheep crosses the stream, it turns colour. The black ones turn
white and the white ones turn black. I tried scuba diving, and
that's also as good as acid, but I figured that Medieval Studies
is, on the whole, a lot less expensive, and marginally less dangerous." Jake started out a Renaissance man but ultimately re-
belled against the worship of Shakespeare and turned his attention to what he called "everything but" — Marlowe, Webster,
Middleton, the dark chaos of revenge tragedy. They completed
their doctorates the same spring, married after living together
for eight years, and moved to a foothills boomtown, where Stella
had a tenure-track position at a burgeoning English Department. Jake toiled on as a sessional for three years before being
hired full-time. It was the infant days of affirmative action, an
injustice and humiliation that he ranted and raved about for
years. His James Dean posturing and outrageous pronouncements received hearty laughs in the early eighties, somewhat
sparser laughter as the decade progressed, and frowns and gasps
of exasperated shock by the time the nineties rolled around.
Student complaints and grievances mounted, and, by 1995, less
than a year after walking out on Stella, Jake had become an
embarrassment and was asked to resign. He received a fairly
generous settlement — enough to live on — and, when Charlotte dumped him, he set up house with his drinking buddies
and joined the Bonk-of-the-Month club. He seems happy, Stella
thinks. Maybe this is what he wanted all along. Last time the
kids mentioned what Dad did with his days, they said he was a
partner in a coffeehouse, making espresso and hosting poetry
readings by ageing Beats.

⌒

Finally emerging from the bush, out into the sunlight, Stella and Stephen fairly dance their way to the top of the hill. Stephen was right — the view is opulent. They sit side by side on the hilltop, hunkered down in wind, shoulders touching, silent. Till Stephen ventures "I'm really getting into Gurdjieff these days. His understanding of human psychology, of sexuality, it's incredibly advanced for his time——"

Stella recognizes this moment. A student, a colleague, a hockey dad in the arena coffee shop — some man mentions pleasure, desire, sexuality — offers an opening. And Stella reacts bodily, far below the level of conscious thought. She deflects, she ducks, she gets the hell out of the way.

A bird flies into her silence — the impossible yellow of a goldfinch flashes above their heads and disappears. Stephen continues, "But another text I really love right now is a Tibetan Buddhist work called the *Dhammapada*. There's a line in there that the enlightened one is like a bird that leaves no trace in the sky."

Stella says, "I just remembered something else Jake taught me. To always acknowledge my sources, as you just did. As you always seem to do. I once described the male genitals as 'turkey neck and turkey gizzards' — and Jake waited a moment to see if I'd give Sylvia Plath the credit, but when I didn't——" With these words, Stella walks through the opening effortlessly, without even planning to.

They gaze out at the green world spread before them. The mound and cleft of the hills is an open invitation. The fringe of cloud on the horizon has thickened, bubbled up, and is moving toward them, through a sky that is quick and alive above their heads. A pungent scent of sage is released by the weight of their bodies. Stephen says, "The Buddhists teach that the reason we're made human is because of our desire. That we're in this incarnation to work through that."

"Do you think so?"

"I'm not sure. I think the problem with desire is that fulfilment doesn't diminish it."

"Neither does denial."

He looks away, ducks his head." You got that right," he murmurs.

It occurs to Stella that, for the second time today, *anything could happen.* They both lift their heads toward the sound of a distant rumbling — thunder? — then Stephen says, "I spend a lot of time at the abbey, talking to the monks. They seem really happy."

"The world's not such a terrible place. No, I'm lying. It sucks ..."

He is silent. The rumbling sound grows louder and more prolonged. Half of the sky is now filled with dark clouds, moving fast. Stella says, "It's coming this way."

"Yeah. We'd better take cover." They stand. It takes Stella a moment to gather her things. She realizes that he is carrying nothing. He stands up and is ready to go. Stella, on the other hand, has her jacket and her enviro-bag from Shop Easy. In it she has her Walkman; a couple of tapes; her wallet, stuffed with bills and coins, credit cards, bank slips, and dozens of frequent-renter/coffee-drinker/book-club cards that she can never find when she needs them. She has her sun visor, her prescription sunglasses, her reading glasses. A couple of Kleenexes. A note pad and pen. A paperback novel. Cigarettes and several packs of matches. She has her yellow-and-white-striped Giorgio bag, a free gift from the Bay with a purchase of twenty-five dollars or more. Inside the Giorgio bag are a toothbrush and toothpaste, a comb, lip balm, skin cream, a couple of hairpins, a tube of After Bite, and one nicotine patch.

Stephen carries nothing, just the clothes on his back. A V-neck T-shirt, such a faded powder blue that it's nearly white. Black cotton trousers (not jeans), black leather walking boots, and a red-on-black lumberjack shirt. Nothing he wears displays a label or logo.

Stephen leads the way down the hill. "Well," Stella says, having learned to feel safer talking to someone's back, "what's the verdict? Blows and wounds? Or wonders?" He stops, turns around to face her, and smiles. "Wonders," he says, and his hand rises to gently trace the curve of her cheek. Stella can't name her reaction as surprise, for she sensed this energy ever since she sat down at his table in the cafeteria — sensed it without recognition. There's a freedom in the way he offers himself, the prospect of nothing but delight. Without even thinking about the huge gap between his words and her assumptions, she blurts: "Stephen, I haven't been anywhere near a man for years."

"I don't ask for anything you can't give or don't want to give."

They have now crested the next ridge and have two choices — the rush and noise of the highway or the road back down to the slough. Stephen gently steers Stella down. His hand slides up from the small of her back to her shoulders. She cautiously slides her arm around his waist. They bump together. "Stephen, how old are you?"

"Twenty-one."

"Jesus."

Silence. They move awkwardly down the hill, and Stella breaks away, stops. He smiles. "Try this," offering his hand. It's a more manageable piece of him, and she turns it over in her own. "You have childlike hands," she says, and shows him hers — red-knuckled, snaked with bluish veins. "I've had elderly hands since I was eighteen. I don't know why."

The benign sky under which they set out is now a uniform

grey overhead, its darkening edges pulling rapidly together, a dark circle closing over their heads. The freedom bubbles up between them. There's no cover, there are no trees here. Just three large stones, placed in a wide triangle, on the flattening bottom of their hilltop. "This looks like a good place," he says, without irony, and they sit side by side on the grass and await the storm.

As the first splatters of rain fall, Stella wriggles close to Stephen, pressing her hip and the length of her leg against his. He reaches for her, enfolds her in his big arms. She feels safe, safe enough to explore him, moving the side of her head languidly against his shoulder. She doesn't trust her hands, not yet; she nuzzles and rubs against him like a cat. He says, over the howl of the wind, "I want to know about you, what your life has been like."

"Well, let's see. I used to be a Marxist, a Deadhead, a druggie, a revolutionary, waitress in a Gastown bar, Forestry worker. God, I sound like one of those author's biographies on the back of a book of self-published poetry ..."

Stella discovers the great pleasure of rubbing the side of her skull, just behind her ear, against the warm roundness of his shoulder.

The splatter of rain thickens, but still they laugh and refuse to move. He takes off his red fleece and wraps it around her shoulders. She fixes her eyes on the brown V of chest and gently lays her hand flat against his breastbone.

Their words and nestling interweave seamlessly, the talk falling away unnoticed in the thrall of a new touch. The storm begins, now — rolls of thunder, flashes of lightning. Despite the jacket, Stella shivers. Stephen is serene, warm, still. Stella pictures the blood coursing smoothly through his unobstructed veins, his big heart steadily thumping, efficient, unabused.

A shiver shakes her, and Stephen laughs and brushes the rain from her face. "You're getting cold, aren't you? Shall we make our way back?" It has become too dark for bushwacking. Besides, they don't want to go back the way they came. When they stand up, when they move apart to resume their journey, when she's not touching him any more, at least not for a moment, a sense of loss washes over Stella. Her body trembles violently at the withdrawal of his warmth. She feels unutterably bereft.

Stella describes herself as cosmetically challenged, and prefers to leave such matters to experts — colouring her hair, facials, eyelash-tinting, brow-shaping, leg-waxing. These are treats and treatments she has learned to give herself since she's been on her own, since she's made tenure. It occurs to her now and then that maintaining her beauty and composure in her forties costs a lot of money, takes a lot of time, and usually involves lying in a darkened room while someone works on her body.

Stella gets a massage once a week. She goes to see a man named Larry Nakamura, who works at her health club. Twenty-five dollars per half-hour and he patiently kneads the kinks in her neck, the tense lumps between her shoulder blades. But what Stella really comes back for is the attention he pays to her hips and behind. She figures that it's worth a hundred bucks a month just to be touched below the waist by big meaty hands. She smiles and sighs into her towelled headrest while Larry murmurs over her hip flexors.

Stella and Stephen are several kilometres from the retreat. They could follow the fence line across the hills and try to meet up with the railway tracks again, or walk the other way, towards the highway. The sound of the highway intimidates Stella —

eq the textbook of the rose

too real, too harsh. "I'm wearing tights, so I can't hike up my skirt like Claudette Colbert in *It Happened One Night.*"

"Is that a movie?"

"Yeah. Let's try following the fence line."

The rain increases in force. Stella has to take her glasses off and immediately feels disoriented and vulnerable. Stephen takes hold of her hand under the black and howling sky; she has no choice but to trust him. After they have trudged along in silence for some time, Stephen says, "I think if we cross right here we'll be able to reach the tracks and just follow them back."

"Okay," she says.

The moment they reach the tracks, the rain stops as suddenly as it came. They clamber through the barbed wire and into the cow pasture. Though they meander, before they know it the building suddenly looms, figures moving before the big picture windows, the cocktail reception following someone's talk — oh God, was it Diana's? Yes, Diana's talk on class and spirituality. The familiar solidity of the building, the voices, repel Stella. The world intrudes, threatens the spell.

Stephen takes her hand and moves purposefully toward the fire-exit door that opens onto the wing of the students' dorm. In ten seconds, they could be inside his room.

"Stephen. No. I can't. "

He sighs gently, enfolds her in his arms, touches her hair. "Sure?"

"Yes. Goodnight." Stella can't. Not now. Not yet. She needs time to collect herself, to think.

Diana passes her in the hallway. "What the hell happened to *you?*"

"I'm not sure," Stella says. "How'd the paper go?"

"My talk, you mean? It was respectfully received. I'm safe here, Stella. So are you."

The rooms at St. Jerome's are extremely small, but Stella's contains, in addition to the meagre furnishings provided, a laptop, monitor, and printer, software, manuals, and paper. A stack of files of current research and department business and course syllabi. A dozen reference books on feminist criticism, spirituality, parenting, and Chaucer. Stella has brought five pairs of shoes and enough clothes to last ten days. An electric fan in case of hot nights, an extra blanket in case of cool ones, her orthopedic pillow, a kettle, a mug, a canister of tea, several large plastic bottles of mineral water (carbonated, flavoured, and plain), four bottles of white wine and a corkscrew, a basket of fresh fruit, a box of crackers, a packet of Gummi Bears. A brass candlestick and scented candle, five-pound wrist weights, a yoga mat and bolster, a hot-water bottle (Stella's hands and feet are always cold — twenty-five years of smoking), as well as an ice pack and tensor bandages.

Stella stands in the familiar jumble, breathing rapidly, muttering, "Jesus. God." Trembling with cold, she squelches out of her shoes, gingerly untying laces prickly with burrs. She wrings out her socks, peels off soaked leggings pierced with thorns; her sweater is smudged with grass stains and mud. There are dead bugs in her hair and faint smears of blood on her skin.

She takes a hot shower and changes into dry clothes. "Jesus, God." Her vocabulary has evaporated. She laughs. The face she sees in the mirror is radiant.


Every other weekend, Zachary and Miranda go to visit their father. On the Friday nights of these sleepover weekends, Stella makes plans to socialize. This is something she puts on her list of things to do: She invites colleagues or neighbours or old friends to dinner, or arranges to see a concert or a play. Stella does this not because it gives her pleasure, but because it is necessary; it is something she should and must do, in order to properly take care of herself.

But every other Saturday night, Stella indulges in the guiltless pleasure of staying home All By Herself. She does not answer the phone. She plays the stereo full blast. She has a long, luxurious bath, by candlelight. She masturbates, using everything from state-of-the-art love-shop technology to root vegetables. Then, anointed with scent and provocatively dressed for bed (no flannel nighties on Saturday nights), she loads a video into the VCR. Usually it's a well-reviewed art film, one that she can discuss with intelligence and animation in the department lounge, or sometimes a Hollywood thriller — but once in a while, actually quite often — more often than she would like to admit — Stella indulges her secret passion for women's movies, the kind that were made in the fifties —*Mildred Pierce, Madame X, Letter to Three Wives, The Women.* She sits on the couch, dabbing moist eyes at the heroic self-sacrifice, the broad and ludicrous gestures of selfless love. After the movie ends, Stella rewinds the tape, pours herself a nightcap, smokes a few more cigarettes, and curls up in a ball on the living-room rug and cries and cries and cries. The ritual has changed, as the years since Jake's departure have passed, from a necessity to a mere habit — to tap into this scarred but familiar vein of betrayed melancholy.

Nigel has left a small brown bag outside her door. It contains a tuna sandwich on brown, a waxy Delicious apple, a plum, and a can of iced tea. Nigel. She must do something about Nigel; she must explain, must say something to him, let him know somehow. Because, Stella realizes, she has already decided what she is going to do.

She should be starved — she has been outside, walking, for

over five hours — but she can't bring herself to eat anything but
the plum. 10:05. She'll wait thirty minutes and if she hasn't
changed her mind ...

Out onto the porch for a smoke. Brushes her teeth. Tries to
read, but the words swim before her eyes, meaningless and trivial.
Tries to stretch, paces. Looks again in the bathroom mirror,
unable to recognize herself.

10:17. Tries to read again. Takes out her Peruvian knapsack
and pops in a few things she might need. The Giorgio bag. The
brass candlestick and scented candle. A condom. Would it be
presumptuous to bring two?

10:21. Another smoke. Brush the teeth again, fluff the still-
damp hair. She can't very well knock on Nigel's door now, can
she? It would feel too much like asking permission.

10:26 Fuck ritual delay. Stella storms down the corridor,
skirting the lounge and going out through the front doors. She
circles the building in the dark — the rain has stopped, but the
wind still howls and chills. A gust of wind up-ends the knapsack, and the condom skitters out of the bag and under a parked
car. Stella crouches on the gravel and strains to retrieve it, leaving the imprint of dozens of tiny pebbles on her knees.

Entering the students' wing through the fire exit closest to
Stephen's room, Stella hesitates, peers down the hall, sees no
one. Knocks. No answer, but voices approach from the far end
of the corridor. She tries his door and it opens. Sumptuous darkness, a form on the bed.

"Stephen."

"Hi."

"I stayed away as long as I could."

*The first time they made love, she mapped her body for him. "These
are what breasts look like after they've nursed children. The skin is*

*there but the flesh inside just drains away." "Beautiful," he says. He tenderly traces an undulating stretch mark with his finger.*

They tumble together at night, excusing themselves — discreetly and separately — from the ball-games and receptions and readings, to meet in his room. Stella brings various items with her — her tape deck and recording of Mozart arias (but Stephen finds opera "distracting"), a basket of fruit, a bottle of sparkling water. Her blow dryer, to help him dry his shoes. At first, Stella slinks away during the night, seeking the sanctuary of her own room. Next morning, if he's not at breakfast, she returns to him, and they make love again. If he is at breakfast, they manufacture some pretext — the loan of a book, the return of a tape — so that they can be alone together again, in his room. On his bed.

Stephen's purity, his lack of blemish, shine from him. When Stella pictures him, draws his image into her mind, even years later, he's bathed in light. A Grail knight. In real life, the illusion comes from his smile. Even in repose, the contours of his face are soft, malleable, ready to be amused, delighted, pleased. She has never heard him swear. He uses the anatomically correct names for all body parts. She has never heard him say that this thing or that thing pisses him off. He doesn't make jokes, but receives them with pleasure. His laugh is frequent but soft, not an explosive guffaw but a light chuckle, rumbling up through his body. She can feel it moving like an aftershock when she's lying on top of him.

Sometimes, she worries that he's not too bright.

He never complains, about anything or anyone. Not about

his parents or siblings or professors or friends. He doesn't talk of former lovers. They'd established risk on that second night, a complete exchange of sexual histories. "You go first," he said. "Yours will take longer."

"If we go back to '68, yes. But since 1980, one — namely, my husband. And a few humiliating gropes on first dates, but that's beside the point. And you?"

"None."

Stella takes a moment to digest this information. "All right then. But don't go mistaking me for the goddess of love, okay?"

"No danger of that, Stella. So, do we need to use these any more?"

Stella calculates that it's about day sixteen. "Nope," she says, and Stephen flicks the foil packet through the air, clang, into the wastebasket. "Shoots, scores!" She laughs, pulling him into her arms.

Sometimes, when he is not with her, Stella says to herself, *Give your head a shake! This guy can't be for real, he's from another planet. This guy is a twenty-one-year-old North American, white, middle-class male. The kind who fill your classrooms, sneering, burping, farting. Sweaty, thick-necked, crunching potato chips. Crude, insolent, aggressive, hostile, dangerous. He's one of those. That's the species he belongs to. Either he's a mutant, or you've been DONE, girl, big time.*

When she's with him, though, Stella forgets the questions she meant to ask, forgets to seek out the cracks in the armour, forgets to force him to disclose himself. Instead, her spirit opens to him; she wants to tell him everything; she makes him a scale drawing of the house she grew up in. And, one night, she tells him the story of Jake and Charlotte. It begins: "This is what I got for my thirty-ninth birthday." Stephen listens and does not speak for a long time. Then he sighs and says, "What a hard, brilliant thing. You'll always carry it with you." Of all the people to whom she has told her story, Stephen is the only one who doesn't expect her to get over it.

Stella did talk to Nigel. She did not do the right thing, but she did the best she could. She drew him aside after dinner, and said, "When I went for that walk with Stephen last night, the strangest thing happened." He looked at her, polite but wary. "I'm sorry," she blustered. "What you said really meant something, it wasn't just nothing. I thought I was just going for a walk and he'd ask for advice about his honours project or his girlfriend. What I'm trying to say is that I wasn't playing games. I like you Nigel, we could write to each other, maybe ..."

"*Write* to each other?"

"This thing with Stephen, it won't last, it'll be over in a few days, I just——"

"Sure thing, Stella. We can write to each other." He walked away. She started to call out "I never meant——" but stopped herself, recalling that Nigel has heard those words before. So has she. Jake also said, "I didn't mean to hurt you," and "I couldn't help it." And, Stella's personal favourite: "Shit happens."

Stephen is lying on his back, hands behind his head. Stella is draped over him, her abdomen against his groin, her head resting in the smooth trough of his ribcage. He says he can feel her heart beating right through him. She sighs. "So this crow lands on the spot of blood on the snow, and there it is, flapping its wings and drinking up the blood. And I've worked with these texts my entire adult life, and I still can't get a handle on the image. I see it in my head all the time."

"What attracts you?"

"The mystery, the recurrence, the meaning of it, I guess."

"Don't you already have a sense of what it means?"

"Well, yes. No. I don't know. It's like Blake's 'The Sick Rose.' You can read it an almost infinite number of ways. You would have liked him, Stephen. You two could have sat in trees together and talked to angels——"

"He talked with angels?"

"At age six. Anyway, maybe it's just like 'The Sick Rose.' Maybe there's no one way to read it, no one way to say what it means. Then again, I usually close my last class on Blake with a reading from his own cosmology that makes it pretty clear he was talking about pure passion destroyed by bourgeois morality——"

"So you don't really leave it up to them."

"No, I guess I don't. I mean, I try to convince them that they're capable of understanding poetry, but you're right, I guess I do lead them to the most logical reading that I've ever found. It's my Apostle's Creed — I believe in God the author, God the book, and God the holy secondary source——"

"So what about the crow on the snow, then?"

"Yeah, what about it? You haven't said. What do you think?"

"Well, there's a parable about that in *The Book of Sufi.*"

"Do you realize you're probably the only person in the world who can say that without sounding pretentious?"

"That's nice. I think it goes, 'Only the bird understands the textbook of the rose.' I don't remember the rest."

Stella traces his rib with her finger, the bone in its case of velvety flesh. Noise in the corridor, light slanting through the threadbare curtains, the day is beginning. Stephen reaches for Stella, and moves his big arms in an arc, raising her up above him like an angel, like a bird.

⌐

On the second night, she straddled him, moving her hips in a circle until he groaned. "Go for it," she whispered, greedy for his pleasure, greedy to go all the way. The next morning, she went to him after breakfast, still asleep at nine, late for his seminar on Ouspensky's London circle. Sliding between the sheets, nestling against him while he nuzzled her neck, Stella allowed his now slow and patient fingers to find and please her, a joyous suffusion that leaves her sprawled against the broad warmth of his chest, laughing with tears in her eyes. Afterwards, she went for a long walk along the railway tracks, mind, body, and soul enfolded in bliss.

By the fourth night, she slept in his arms, as he'd asked her to do from the beginning. It no longer seemed necessary to reclaim herself, to get out the chalk and redraw the boundaries. She was safe where she was.

The next morning, Stella awoke with the warmth of his breath on the back of her neck, his sweat evaporating on her thighs. She stretched, sighed, and heard him say, "I have to leave tonight."

"You do? Why? The retreat doesn't end till tomorrow!"

"It's the only time I could get a ride back to the abbey."

"With someone from here?"

"No. My mother is picking me up."

At four, when her seminar is over, she can't find Stephen anywhere. They have so little time left. Where is he? His room is empty, the bed stripped, his suitcase packed and ready. Stella makes several furtive and shamefaced trips to his room, each time retrieving an item or two of her detritus — the blow dryer, a tape, a book, a poem. Of course she mothered the guy; it's the only kind of love she's ever shown any aptitude for. Her spirit hurts, the stone blossoms in her chest, her shoulder muscles ache and contract. Where is he? Look at the time. We're running out of time.

He finds her at six, says he got shanghaied by his study group into a hike that went longer than planned. Stella's bed is littered with books, papers, and cardboard boxes. "Let's go for a walk," she says.

He takes her hand as soon as they're out of sight of the buildings. She says, "I was so afraid you'd leave without saying goodbye." It occurs to her that she has lived entirely free of dread for days now, and she notices the misery of its sudden clench — she's afraid of never seeing him again, afraid that she's made a fool of herself, afraid that he has made a fool of her, afraid that this was a mistake, that he regrets everything, that he's ashamed, that she'll never lay her hand on his warm brown chest again ...

Hands linked, they climb to the top of a hill near the retreat. The sun is out, but a brisk wind is blowing, and they sit close together, scrunched down in the wind. He begins to chatter, inanely. About a dog he used to have. About a famous aikido master who defeated opponents in slow motion. About fainting spells. They come unbidden, Stephen says. No, never during a kick-boxing match, just at strange, unpredictable times. Lifting a cardboard box, starting a lawn mower. Stephen says that he went to a specialist, who hooked him up to some kind of brain scanner. Stephen had to put on glasses that distorted everything, that flashed bright lights into his eyes, to see if he'd have a seizure. He didn't. He laughs, "So I wasn't epileptic, but they measured my brain waves on this graph, and they were really ... flat. Low. I guess most people's brain waves zigzag up and down like mad, but my line was just——"

"Hi, Stella and Stephen!" Voices, tinged with high spirits and generous laughter call to them from another hill. A group of retreatants, out for an after-dinner stroll. Everybody knows. It doesn't matter. They spread Stella's jacket on the ground and lie side by side, stiffly, like figures on a sarcophagus. After a while, he says, "Would you lie on my back, like the other night?" He rolls over onto his stomach and stretches out on the ground. Stella climbs on top of him, feeling her breasts crushed against the muscles of his back, her hips curved against his backside, like nested spoons. He warms her, it's lovely, her back open to waning sun and chill breeze while his warmth rises through her. When he leans up on his elbows to speak, his shoulder blades pillow her head. He says, "I don't want you to suffer."

"You delighted me. You gave me my body back."

"I wanted your body." He starts to say more, but Stella stops him right there.

"Good. So did I."

Parting is excruciating, comical, painful, and abrupt. Stella recognizes his mother the moment she walks into the lounge — a sturdy middle-aged woman with short greying hair, walking shoes, and a Tilley hat. When Stephen moves toward the door, Stella slinks off down the corridor to her room. A soft knock comes a moment later, and there stands Stephen with her brass candlestick in his outstretched hand. A hurried embrace: "Goodbye, Stephen," she says and turns away, closing her door. Dear God, she thinks, reeling with shame. Dear God.

The next morning, at breakfast, Stella is quiet, and Nigel says, "Come for a walk with me." The dew still sparkles on the grass, and Stella's dime-store thongs slide and slip as they try to climb the small hill outside her dorm — but they give up, and settle for a spot a short way up. "So, how are you doing?" Nigel asks. Grateful, Stella says, "I'm trying to cultivate detachment." Nigel throws an arm awkwardly over her shoulder, a familiar gesture of desire tinged with fear. But Stella has received the gift, from Stephen, of reclaiming her body, and with a quick nestling, she fits herself alongside Nigel, slots her hip against his thigh, feels the muscle deep inside the hip bone that had tingled under Stephen's hands only hours before. So she comforts Nigel, and herself; he accepts this gift from her, and they sit in silence together, watching the August morning gather its fierce heat, until honking horns in the parking lot remind them that it's time to go home.

Stella returns to her real life reluctantly, sadly, but wearing an unconscious aura of sexual contentment that seems to emit a primal scent. Even the man at the car wash suddenly begs her for a date. He's been washing her car, emptying the ashtrays, vacuuming up the gum wrappers, retrieving missing library books and amputated legs of action heroes for years — but he's never asked her out before. Stella smiles at him, and politely declines.

The lust wears off first, after a week or two. It's the longing that's harder to shake. In her bed at night, or gazing at the moon while sneaking a last smoke on the porch. She writes Stephen a letter. A friendly, undemanding letter, devoid of presumption. Telling him how much she loved being with him. How, when she thinks of him, she smiles. Nothing more, just the eloquence of her return address on the envelope. She thinks it over for a day or two, walking around with the stamped letter in her briefcase.

On a morning in early September, exactly one month after their walk to the hill of wonders, Stella just lets him go. Decides that she doesn't need him, is content without him, is simply glad she met him. She tears up the unmailed letter.

Toward the end of September, Stella notices that she feels funny, is gaining weight, and hasn't menstruated for a while. *The blue line in the big window means your test is ready. A blue line in the small window means you are pregnant.*

Her first thought is to just dispose of it without a word to anyone. She's seen those ads under "Family Planning" in the Yellow Pages. A quick drive across the line, make a weekend of it, that Going To the Sun highway is supposed to be spectacular. She will not go to her GP, she will not go to her gynaecologist. She most definitely will not go to the clinic, the converted drycleaners' across from the Esso Station. She will not brave the deranged protesters with their dayglo signs and photographs of garbage bins, dumpsters, full of foetal body parts, tiny heads, greyish bloodied fingers, twisted legs.

No. Stephen is an honourable man, she still believes this, and to dishonour him would be shameful. She will tell him and they will agree that this is an unfortunate mistake. The letter is difficult to compose. "Stephen, I'm too old to have another child. I have too many children already, Stephen. I can't raise another child on my own, I'm too tired." While Stella struggles to write the letter, a secret fantasy arises in her mind. Stella's secret fantasy is that he will say, "Why do you have to raise this child on your own?" Stella's secret fantasy, which attracts and horrifies her so deeply that she has to ration the amount of time she allows herself to dream it each day, goes like this:

*Stella packs in the department, gets a sessional teaching job at some little community college in the mountains. She cashes in her RRSPs, and puts that money, and the equity from her house, into an old farm near a lake. She and her children and Stephen and their child live there together. Stella teaches at the college, Stephen cares for the child. The older children cheerfully march off each morning down a fruit-tree-shaded lane to catch the school bus. After school, Stephen teaches them t'ai chi. He teaches them that being a man does not mean being a bully. The children adore him. Their garden is huge and prodigal. Stella makes apple chutney, green-tomato relish, pies. Eden. On midsummer evenings Stella spreads a checkered cloth on the ground in the orchard, while the little one toddles among the plum trees, holding Miranda's hand, and Stephen plays catch with Zak, the gentle thud of the softball dropping into the glove ...*

Stella just can't seem to get the letter right. She's about eight weeks now, and she can't stay pregnant much longer. The longer she stays pregnant, the harder it will be to put an end to it. Stella knows what this choice entails, knows what is being lost. She's not eighteen any more.

So she phones him. Fortified by a shot of Jack Daniels, she calls directory one Sunday evening and gets a number. She dials, and Stephen answers. He sounds pleased to hear from her: "I've been thinking of you. How are you?"

"Not so good. Stephen, we have a problem. I'm pregnant."

"I thought — I mean — oh, that time. I'm so surprised."

"You think *you're* surprised? Stephen, I can't have this baby."

"We need to talk. Can I come to see you? I can miss a few classes."

On a Tuesday afternoon in the first week of October, Stella and her kids pull up to the curb in front of her house, and Zachary mutters "Who the hell is that?" Stephen is standing on the front porch, smiling. There is nothing in his hands.

His presence is a balm. The children overcome their usual suspicions in record time. Their normal pattern with friends and suitors is early excessive politeness, followed, usually within a week, by pugnacious rudeness and testing.

"This is my friend Stephen," Stella tells them. "He'll be staying with us for a while."

The pantomime of having him sleep on the hide-a-bed in the basement is dispensed with after two days. "How do you feel about Stephen staying in Mommy's bed?"

"Fine," says Miranda. "Okay," says Zak.

Stephen doesn't court them or ignore them or really do anything at all. But they draw to him, as if they can't help themselves. Zachary stands at the patio door, watching Stephen move. "What're you doing?"

"It's called t'ai chi."

"Do you have a black belt? Are you a ninja?"

"There are no belts. It's not like karate."

"What is it like, then?"

"Come out and I'll show you."

The harangues that Stella has rehearsed are unnecessary: "See how I live, see what my life is like, see how exhausted and stretched thin I am, you can't possibly expect me, at my age — and if you insist on this, you must agree to take full responsibility, you must agree not to abandon me, not to betray me, not to——"

At night, their lovemaking takes on a leisurely lushness; they now have all the time in the world. Their lovemaking goes so deep that Stella drifts through her workday as though her body, her thighs, her skull, are filled with air instead of flesh and bone. They make love all through their nights, going to bed the moment the lights go out in the children's rooms.

After Jake left, Stella's children began to wake during the night, wander downstairs, and crawl into her bed. A psychologist friend suggested that they did this to make sure that she was still there. But once Stephen arrives, Zak and Miranda begin to sleep soundly through the night. Without protest, sulks, or comment, they simply get up when their alarm rings and go straight to the kitchen, to their bowls of cereal and glasses of juice. And Stella begins to wonder whether her friend was right, or whether Zak and Miranda just wanted to make sure she wasn't alone any more.

*The loathly lady offers Peredur a choice. She can be lovely and young only in the daytime or only at night. Peredur chooses to have her lovely for himself alone. His reward for not caring for the opinion of the world is, of course, to have his lady lovely all the time.*

Stephen has stayed two weeks, and, one morning, he announces that he has to leave, has to return to his classes and obligations. They both have already decided, not with any discussion but rather in silent assent, that this child will be born, that they will raise it together.

"I'll come back at Christmas break," Stephen says.

"All right."

"And then I'll be finished my degree in April. Before the baby comes."

"Yes."

This second goodbye is not nearly as hard as the first. Stella has faith. She has kept him pretty much under wraps for the past two weeks, and when colleagues comment on her cheerfulness, her glowing skin, her expanding waistline, she announces, "Oh, I quit smoking."

And she has. Stephen never said a word, but every time she went to light up — claiming stress anxiety worry — she'd usually just stub the thing out after a puff or two, forgetting why she wanted it in the first place.

At the end of November, the amnio results come. The baby is fine. She calls Stephen to tell him the good news. She calls and calls. She tries early in the morning, she tries late in the evening. After three days, she calls him in the middle of the night. The phone rings and rings and rings. Stephen does not answer.

After eight days and nights, Stella calls the Religious Studies Department, masquerades as one of his English professors, makes up a story about how he's been absent from classes and has an overdue term paper. The secretary says, "Stephen Harding? I thought we'd contacted all his profs, we sent out a memo——"

"I must have missed mine."

"Well, he died. About two weeks ago. It was very sudden. A brain aneurysm."

"Was it— Was he——"

"He was just walking home from classes, one afternoon. Stephen was very highly regarded here. We've started a memorial scholarship fund, if you'd care to make a donation."

Darkness. Stella in a dark room. Full ashtray, nearly empty bottle. _The Mabinogion._ Ovid's _Metamorphoses._ Leonard Cohen intoning doom on the stereo, the volume turned low. Nothing works, though. Nothing numbs enough, nothing stills it. Jack Daniels, half a bottle of Tylenol, nothing helps. Retreat/no exit.

Orange dayglo letters. In the flick of the lighter's flame, the Yellow Pages. Family Planning. Nineteen weeks. *It takes about two hours to kill a baby this way;* that's what the pamphlets say. Fire out. The machine clicks and it's the Allman Brothers, "Not My Cross to Bear," Gregg's husky tenor insinuating itself around his brother's guitar, symbiosis ... the perfection of heartache. Stella has done her research, she found his hometown paper, she has a photocopy of the death notice before her. In black and white. "Suddenly, on November 3rd, 1997, at the age of 21 ..." There is no way out of the darkness, she knows. In the old tale, the grieving goddess reproaches the Fates, and swears to the fallen Adonis, *Your blood shall be changed into a flower; that consolation none can envy me.*

Stephen and Stella are lost. A tangle of bushes, the motionless fetid slough, edges crazily mud-sculptured by trampling hooves of unseen cattle. They can't even see the hill of wonders from here, it might as well be a dream.

This is their fourth attempt to leave the pathless forest. They are tired, footsore, discouraged. Stella is hungry and thirsty, she's missed dinner, she's been walking for hours. Her leggings are pricked with burrs. Ravening mosquitoes dive-bomb her, whining and furious. The mosquitoes have translucent striped bellies, through which the blood is visible. A swat leaves a spatter the size of a dime. Stella wipes her own blood from her hands and peers through the dense bush. Crows squawk invisibly in the trees overhead, raucous and scornful. But it looks to her as if the slough ends just over there, across a small creek. "Let's try that way," she says.

"All right."

She catches a glimpse of a cowpath that skirts the slough, just on the other side, smacks a mosquito that has already drawn blood from her temple. "We can jump here," she says. "I hate to turn back now that we've come this far." Stella gathers her strength, vaults across the muddy creek, lands neatly on the other side, smiles, and reaches out her hand.

Two women in late middle age sit together on a screened porch, content in each other's company, watching a child of about two intent with his crayons. A fiery sunset burns before them, the sun a furious red ball, reddening as it sinks, drawing with it, slowly, the stunning heat of the prairie day. Crickets, sensing the coming coolness, tentatively begin to sing.

The women sip tall gin-and-tonics. They have agreed that quitting smoking is tough, and staying quit is even tougher, but worth it in the long run. They have exhausted the topic of menopause. They agree that the elimination of caffeine and refined sugar is essential, but Margaret is politely dismissive of Stella's enthusiasm for Chinese herbs, while Stella urges Margaret never to succumb to hormone replacement. They have discussed retirement — Stella's early retirement package of three years ago, the settlement Margaret will receive from her school board next year in 2001. Perhaps, they laugh, they'll pool their money, buy a Winnebago, drink lots of gin, wear baggy Bermuda shorts, and play bridge and be godawful loud tourists, complaining about the bugs and the waitresses and the prices all up and down the North American coasts. Post-menopausal retirees run wild. They giggle, but, at the same moment, glance over at the child.

Stella says, "It's all right. I'm happy. Of course I miss Stephen, but — I mean, my loss is nowhere near yours. Oh hell———"

"It's all right," Margaret says. "I understand. Tell me about the conference."

"Oh, it's the annual Medieval Studies Association thing.

Lots of eager grad students and familiar old bores."

"And you're giving a paper?"

"Yes. It's on the prepatriarchal goddess figure, variously named Hera, Isis, Aphrodite, Stella Maris aka Star of the Sea. She survived in various subversive forms into the Middle Ages. Before the Inquisition, before the witch-burnings. My paper looks at the figure of her ... consort. Husband, son, lover. A man much younger than she is. Sometimes called Adonis, Baal, Osiris. I'm looking at the conventions surrounding his death, the laments and dirges, the regeneration that grows out of the mourning——" Stella stops. Her face flushes.

"Sounds interesting," Margaret says.

"Anyhow, I really appreciate your taking the little guy. With Miranda off to camp and Zak spending the summer with his dad, I just——"

"Oh, I'm happy to have him. It's like having my son back again." The child peers with obvious satisfaction at the drawing he has made. "Mommy, Gamma, yook." He carries it over to the women, proudly — a monstrous black dragon-bird, blood dripping from its talons and fangs. Margaret lays her hand gently on the child's head. "I'm so glad to have him," she says.

Stella teaches as a sessional now, at the community college. Full teaching load, but no committees, no grad students, and department meetings are optional. Stella's first children's novel has done well; it's even won an award. It's called *The Textbook of the Rose* and it's about an orphan girl wandering twelfth-century England in search of a home, which she eventually finds in a Franciscan monastery, where she is taught how to read and write. Stella is hard at work on the sequel. Her colleagues at the university thought she'd lost her mind. That chintzy settlement package — it must have been the personal tragedy that unhinged her, the shameful elderly pregnancy, the apparently fatherless child.

Stella sold her tasteful character home in an inner-city neighbourhood and bought a cheaper place close to the college — actually just a mile or two from the old house, but similar layout, half the price. Her new neighbours number not a lawyer, doctor, or accountant among them. There are single moms on welfare living communally in the old two-storey across the road. Berta is a wonderful dayhome provider, and Janet's eldest daughter babysits on weekends. There are quite a few retired couples on the block, too, tending their gardens, content in their empty nests. And students renting basement suites, and young couples in starter homes, with their high-tech baby gear and their dreams. Stella likes it there.

She keeps in touch with Nigel on e-mail. He got a huge research fellowship a couple of years ago, and while doing field work in the Sudan, fell deeply in love with a prof from the host university. Her name is Mbele, she has the carved, calm features of a totem, she is six foot one, regal, good-natured, and the most kindred soul Nigel has ever known. The relationship is long-distance at the moment, but negotiations are in progress.

Stella doesn't have to plan her social life any more, it just happens. She gets invitations from co-workers, or students, or neighbours, or the people in her book club. She has a man in her life, now, too. His name is Percy; he's a medievalist in the History Department, a couple of years younger, but also divorced. When Percy was twelve, he sneaked into Festival Express 70, saw the Dead play with Janis Joplin, her last live concert before she died. He's also familiar with the plot of *It Happened One Night*. Percy's a nice man, good sense of humour. Plays the lute, of all things, and on Tuesday nights he goes Morris dancing.

*PASSUS SEVEN*

MEMORIAM
November 1997

The obituary reads:

> Genereux (Dawson), Delores. Née Tarnowsky. Also
> known as Delia. Died suddenly November 3, 1997, at
> the age of 35. Survived by her mother, Shirley Tarnowsky,
> and Shirley's friend Bob Shoates of Longview, and by
> her son, David, of Port Coquitlam. Also by her sister,
> Marlene, and husband, Randy Sawatsky, and their five
> children, Nacusp. And by her father, Leo Tarnowsky, and
> his wife, Bridget, Fort McMurray. Predeceased by her
> older brother in 1978. A memorial service will be held
> at the Floral Chapel Northeast, 2PM, Monday, Novem-
> ber 6. In lieu of flowers, donations to AADAC would be
> appreciated.

Jake likes reading the obits, likes piecing together the story —
cause of death, success of marriages, number of souls who loved
the deceased. He always feels sorry for the childless ones, especially when the obit's padded with the names of nieces and nephews.

This is an interesting one. No husband; parents split; she's
the second child of this family to die; they've only got one child
left, but at least a prolific one. And what was the dead woman's

kid doing in B.C. if she died here? AADAC ain't the asthma society, that's for sure. It takes several moments for Jake to realize that he knows this woman.

Because he remembers Delia, The Deal, sitting at the kitchen table at Union Street, the night after her brother's funeral. She and Jake had just killed a bottle of cheap sherry between them: "444," the stuff was called. Jake was pissed that Stella had taken off to the Gastown Inn with some bogus gypsy — "Christalmighty, a bandana and one earring and she's so juiced it's embarrassing——" And Deals was pissed off too. She said, "So we had this big twenty-first birthday party for him, it was wild, but he had to go to work the next morning and he was so tired, so hung over, he just passed out. So these assholes, these jerks, they just left my brother lying there on his back. If they'd only turned him over on his stomach, he would've been fine, but they just left him lying there and he choked to death on his own spew...."

These days, Jake makes a point of speaking to his ex-wife as rarely as possible, but he picks up the phone then and there.

"Stella," he says, "listen. The Deal went down. For good."

Doing The Deal, The Deal goes down— aka "Delia," real name the more pedestrian "Delores." The Deal went down on pretty much whoever asked. Everybody did The Deal.

She was beautiful. A tall, slim brunette, big brown eyes, pale skin, Rossetti's Beata Beatrice in patched denim and plaid flannel. Jake called her a Pre-Raphaelite woman once; she thought it was an insult. She was just around during those days on Union Street, just part of the scene.

Jake did The Deal too. Lots of times. She gave him a dose.

The last time he saw The Deal was at the hospital, two days after Miranda was born. Zak was back at home with Grandma, just Stella and Jake and the new baby, officially bonding. Jake had gone down the corridor to check the line-up in the sitz-bath room and, on his way back, glimpsed The Deal up ahead, mincing down the hall. How does she do it, he wondered, how does she just waltz past the nurses like that? The maternity ward is restricted, fathers and sibs only, but there she was, prancing into Stella's room——

"So he shoves me down in the parking lot, I'm screaming my head off, this bunch of people comes running over — hey, Jake. I was just telling Stels how I got this lovely face."

Deals has dressed with care for this visit. A pressed white cotton blouse, a slim khaki skirt with shiny red belt. Royal blue cowboy boots, silver hoops the size of canning seals in her ears, dark hair brushed back and tied with a floral scarf. The left side of Deals's face is purplish black, the skin on her cheek scabbed over in a dark rectangular patch the size of a box of matches.

"So, here to welcome the new arrival?" Jake says, the hearty host, noticing the wince on Stella's face, the flush of sweat on her upper lip. She shifts her behind miserably, no doubt trying desperately to suppress a fart. Her milk is coming in, the Blue Day will be here by tomorrow. She'll cry for twelve hours or so, she'll say *I can't do this. I'm a terrible mother.* And on the fourth day, he will bring his wife and daughter home.

Deals gives the bassinet a cursory glance. "A girl, huh? Great."

Deals announces, proudly, "I took the bus all the way here. The number 10, then transferred to Circle Route."

Deals says, "Here, I made you a plant." She hands Jake a cutting of coleus, plunked crookedly into a Mexican-themed flowerpot heavy with drenched potting soil.

"Thanks, Deals," Jake says. "Only God can make a tree."

Deals continues her story: "So this bunch of people call the cops, and Sharvin or whatever the hell his name is backs off, and they help me up, we end up going back into the bar and the bartender makes up an ice pack for my face. We partied all night, went back to their place, one of the guys says, 'I like to turn you out' but hey, no way, I don't do that shit, so——"

Jake asks, "How are you doing, Stel? Are you wanting to nurse?"

Miranda sleeps soundly. Stella's voice is extremely thin; she looks too exhausted to be alive. "Yes, I think I might."

So it's up to Jake. "Listen, Deals, thanks so much for coming by, but Stella really needs to get her rest. I'll walk you out to the elevators, okay? "

The plant didn't make it, but Stella still has the Mexican flowerpot. It sits on top of the toilet tank over at her place, full of toothbrushes, tubes of toothpaste, plastic containers of flavoured dental floss: mint, grape, bubblegum.

When Stella and Jake left Union Street and moved into student housing, they gradually lost touch with The Deal, with that whole scene. And then they came out west to teach. People from Union Street passed through town now and then, bringing news. Deals landed herself in detox. Deals was really getting her shit together, had a child, got a job, got married. Deals got two years for trafficking. She kind of bounced back and forth between the coast and the prairies, even went up north for a while. She came through town when Stella was about six months pregnant with Miranda. She kept calling, dropping by. Jake noticed how it rattled him, how it rattled Stella, to have someone just show up on their doorstep. It was the first time he'd noticed that no one he knew ever dropped by any more. Dropping by used to be the foundation of social life, just wandering into a place and seeing what was up. (That's how Deals came to Union Street, a fourteen-year-old runaway who heard the music blaring from the open windows, walked in, and said

*Hey, how's it goin'?* That summer Deals got a job at the Forestry
nursery on the Island, came back at the end of the season just in
time for the Dead concert. It was Deals who pointed Stella out
to him that night at the Coliseum, said, *She's good folks. Smart
like you.*) It bothered Jake, then, that he couldn't remember the
last time he'd dropped in on anyone, or anyone had dropped in
on them. In grad school, the flow was constant: people showing up day or night, crackling with a new idea, or stupefied by
romance. And when Jake and Stella bought their first house,
there'd be a Sunday caller, someone to watch the game or have
a beer. But once they had the kids even prearranged visitors
became an imposition.

To Stella at least. She seemed to have just barely enough
energy to mother and work. The first few weeks with his baby
son at home, Jake just wanted to party. *They're here, they're alive,
come look at this beautiful boy we made.* He wanted to invite
everyone he'd ever met.

"Read my lips. No visitors," Stella shrieked at him one night,
an unrecognizable shrew, a banshee. She was right in his face,
screaming "Don't you *get* it? I have to concentrate, here, I have
to pay attention. Don't you understand that anything bad that
happens to this child, for the rest of his life, will be my fault? If
he falls down the stairs, if he gets some disease, if you back over
him in the driveway——"

"Stella, we don't even have a driveway——"

"If a stranger abducts him and rapes him and chops his
body up and scatters the pieces in the woods, the question is
always exactly the same — *but where was the mother?*"

Jake knew enough to take his time, count to ten before
venturing, "So you fart uncontrollably right now, it'll pass, it's
nothing to be embarrassed about. Things get loosened up in
there, but the muscle tone will come back——"

"Fuck off, Jake. Leave me alone."

So he did. If he wanted company, he went out. As the years

passed, he began to feel like a bit player. It was as if Stella had this brass ring in her hand and refused to let it go. She had to have the full meal deal and Jake began to see himself as merely part of the package, and not the best part. Not the fried chicken, not the gravy, not even the fries. No, he was the little Styrofoam container of coleslaw. Or maybe the roll.

Stella paid a duty call to The Deal a few weeks before Miranda was born. Deals had learned to call first, at least. Jake heard his wife mumbling into the phone, "Well, that's not really convenient right now, we're doing a renovation for the baby's room.... A renovation.... Well, yeah, I guess I could. Okay ... Around two? ... What's the address?"

That night, Stella was rigid with fury, slamming pots and pans in the kitchen sink. Jake asked, "So how was tea with Delia?"

"Oh, she told me all about the great guy she met at Narcotics Anonymous. Best sex she's ever had, and he's only beaten her up once. She's into multilevel marketing now, enzymatically alive green foods, only fifty bucks a month for the glow of perfect health. She wants to sign me up, she just needs three more distributors to get to bronze level and qualify for an Escort sedan, if her upline doesn't screw her again, that is. And oh yes, she said, 'My God, Stella you look so much older. I haven't changed at all, I still look exactly the same.'"

"And does she?"

"Yes, Jake, she does." He considered walking over to his wife, kissing the back of her neck, telling her she's still beautiful to him. But they're past that by now, such sitcom tenderness could only be offered ironically, and even then would be met with contempt.

That night, Stella sat up in bed, the baby visibly rolling and

146

kicking at the journal propped on her stomach. She scribbled furiously, then sighed and heaved her bulk out of bed for the ninth or tenth time that evening. Jake leaned over to call out "Careful, the seat's up" and his glance rested on the page where she'd written:

> It's not fair.
> I am *not* like her.

At the front of the funeral chapel, a lavish bouquet sits on a cherrywood table next to an enlarged snapshot of The Deal. Her cascade of dark hair, the porcelain-doll face, almond eyes, impish grin. Propped against the table is a lurid wreath, circled by a purple ribbon with the words "Darling girl" in Gothic gold lettering. Stella got here first. Jake can see her up ahead, across the aisle. The family has the first pew, and it's a sparse gathering. Then there are six empty rows, the rest of the mourners cringing near the back, not wanting to get too close, not wanting to lay claim to this murky death, this carelessly discarded life.

When Jake first walked into the chapel, a burly man in his fifties stopped him at the door. "May I ask your name?"

Jake gave it.

"Wait here, please."

The burly man strode importantly to the front of the church, and spoke to a woman in the front row. The woman turned back to look at Jake, then nodded. The man returned, whispered, "Go ahead. Sit anywhere you like. It's just some undesirables we're concerned about, the people who were with her when she died."

"I see. Of course. Thanks."

Jake studies the memorial booklet while the remaining

mourners file in. He is relieved to see that no religious music or Bible readings or prayers are planned. The Deal has at least been spared that. The minister who stands before them appears to wish fervently that he were elsewhere. He speaks of "Dee," how much she loved animals, how much she loved music. The family has prepared a tape of "Della's" favourite songs, and would be pleased if everyone would join in and sing along. A tape rewinds audibly in the loudspeakers, then Randy Travis's voice, speeded up to a cartoon squeak, washes over the room. "*Foreveraneveramen.*" The tape stops. No one laughs. The tape rewinds loudly, and the song begins again. Still twice the desired speed. The tape races on and on, heads turn toward the back of the room, people fidget in their funeral ensembles, glance down at the booklet in their hands. A snapshot of The Deal on horseback out at the ranch owned by her mother's current boyfriend, the man who shook Jake down at the door. A snapshot of The Deal leaning on a fence at her sister's place in the Kootenays, surrounded prettily by her nieces and nephews. No photo of Deals with her own child, though.

The tape, mercifully, finally, squeals to a halt. A funeral-home official, sweat beading on his forehead, hustles down the centre aisle and speaks *sotto voce* to the minister, who nods solemnly. The official disappears once again through the rear doors of the chapel, while the congregation rustles and coughs and waits. The tape rolls once again, different song; this must be the second song on the program, "Dust in the Wind," a song that is even funnier at double speed than the one before. A woman's voice wails from the front, it's Deals's sister, "No, they're screwing it up, this is terrible!" Delia's mother leans against her sturdy son-in-law and weeps loudly.

The sound of rewinding tape booms through the loudspeakers. There is a blast of feedback, a hum of white noise. It feels hallucinatory, all of it. Jake can't help thinking that The Deal would love this, love looking at the lot of them sweating in that chapel, too ashamed and scared to laugh or move or speak, just waiting for someone to tell them what to do. After what seems an eternity, an unseen hand finds the right switch and the last verse of the song plays through the speakers at the right speed. This catches the mourners off guard, and no one attempts to sing.

The minister stands up, looking even more weary than before. He mentions once again how "Delilah" was loved by all who knew her, how beautiful she was, how much she loved animals. All kinds of animals — horses, dogs, cats. Rabbits. Hamsters, even. "Del's" mother said that she was forever bringing home strays.

The chapel is full of strays. Hard-faced young women, their funereal best consisting of skimpy sundresses covered by cheap acrylic sweaters or Thrift Store ski jackets. The woman next to Jake has removed her ski jacket, the collective embarrassment having raised the temperature in the chapel at least ten degrees. A tattoo on her bicep says, succinctly, "Sex and Violence." Lots of long-haired men, too. The older ones look like bottle pickers; the younger ones have that kind of shagged hair that went out of style in the late seventies, the kind of hair that goes with high-heeled shitkickers and tight pants.

The minister introduces The Deal's sister, who has written a poem in Deals's memory. It is a very bad poem, but feelingly delivered. With an audible sigh of relief, the minister then asks the congregation to rise. He says that the last song will be whatever the tape recorder happens to play. He says that if we're lucky, perhaps the electronic gods will cooperate. He says, *Let's all just hope for the best.*

The loudspeakers squeal, blip, and Sweet Jesus, yes, Bette Midler's throaty voice emerges, at the right speed, singing "The Rose."

The voices are ragged and tentative at first, as the mourners search their programs for the lyrics. It's a ludicrous song, Jake thinks. He knows Stella hates it, but he can hear her, three rows ahead, singing off key but with conviction. Jake, too, raises his own voice manfully, purposefully, around the insipid lyrics. The soprano of Deals's sister floats above them all, clear and sweet. Jake remembers that voice from a bonfire at Jericho Beach, from an into-the-night jam at Union Street.

The post-funeral reception is held in the basement of a modest bungalow near the chapel. The rec room is decorated in a nautical theme. The handrails on the stairs are made of thick hemp cable, the walls decorated with ship's wheels and lithographs of Bluenose schooners. Beer and highballs are served at the wet bar. A card table holds plates of plump and surprisingly tasty sandwiches.

The bungalow belongs to the sister of the current boyfriend of Deals's mother, Shirley. All the connections of the mourners are like that — distant, tentative, complicated. Jake explains, "Well, I'm an old friend. Actually my ex-wife was a close friend of The Deal's, and I just——" And the person he's speaking to turns out to be the cousin of Deals's former boyfriend, only met her a few times, but liked her very much. Or the person is the assistant manager of the video store where Shirley once worked for a few months, actually never met the deceased, but thinks Shirley a great gal, such a terrible blow.

Somebody tells Jake that, no, Deals's son didn't attend. His foster mother couldn't see the point. The child doesn't remember his mother at all, hasn't lived with her since he was eighteen months old, and hasn't seen her since he was three. He was diagnosed with foetal alcohol syndrome when he started Grade One last year, so, between that and the ADD, he's pretty well unadoptable. Shirley says the foster parents are real Bible thumpers, but on the whole seem to treat him pretty good.

Someone else tells Jake that The Deal's current boyfriend was given a day pass to attend the funeral, but had to go back to jail immediately after, so he's not at the reception. Jake saw him enter the church with his escort, the cuffs softly clanking beneath the Mountie's trenchcoat and the oversized sports jacket someone had lent the young prisoner for this occasion. The boy did not weep. Jake doesn't believe he sang either.

It's Marlene, The Deal's sister, who tells him how it happened: "She was doing so great. She called Mom and Bob the day they left to go to Vegas. Her probation was nearly up and she said, 'Don't worry, I'm being really good.' She told them to listen to the radio: she'd requested a song for them, for the road. They never heard it, though. So, afterwards, Mom phoned the radio station and made them check back through all the requests for that day, she just had to know. It was 'Forever and Ever Amen.' Randy Travis."

Stella and Jake successfully avoid each other throughout the proceedings, but when he goes to the foot of the stairs to say his parting words to Delia's mother, he realizes too late that the woman in the navy blue suit just ahead of him is Stella. The mother has Stella crushed against her in a tearful embrace. Shirley glances at him over the shoulder of his ex-wife, and cries, "Oh, and I remember you too, the two of you. And both of you professors now, and a lovely family, she told me."

Neither of them has the heart to disenchant her. They murmur the appropriate phrases — *such a sad thing, a terrible shock, so sorry, so sorry for your loss* — and trudge up the nautical staircase and out of the house together. Stella's face is rigid, unreadable. They do not speak to each other until they are out on the curb, their car keys in hand.

Jake waits. Stella takes a deep breath and says, "So, I'll have the kids ready to go by six o'clock Friday, then."

Of course. There is no more than that. Jake breathes out. "Yes. Okay. Fine."

Jake gets into his car, wondering why the most vivid memory of the day is the feel of the foam cups of Shirley's bra against his chest, her smell of menthol cigarettes and Avon cologne. He wonders why he seems doomed to always remember the wrong things.

He remembers the day he told Stella about him and Charlotte. He wanted to hear her cry "How could you do this to me?" but she didn't. She shouted: "How could you do this to *them*?" It hurt worse than anything that came before or after to know beyond doubt that it wasn't about the two of them any more, hadn't been for years.

He pictures Shirley clutching a phone, pleading with some silky-voiced disc jockey, *Please, just take the time to check. It's important. Please.* Jake wants to go back inside, take the woman's hands in his own and say something, he doesn't know what. Something about Delia's generous spirit, maybe. Or maybe: *The difference is mere gloss.*

He watches Stella climb into her Volvo and drive away. You don't live with a woman for seventeen years without learning a thing or two, and right now Jake knows exactly what she's thinking:

*I am not like her.*
*It's not fair.*

# CODA

## THE TEXTBOOK OF THE ROSE
### November 1999

Two years after Delia's funeral, and it's the last session of Stella's 200-level survey class before fall reading break. They're finishing up *The Canterbury Tales* today, and as always, Stella returns to the Wife of Bath. She says, "I want to draw your attention to the often overlooked fact that the Wife's tale of Sir Gawain and the loathly lady has two endings. Everyone remembers the lovely-all-the-time finale, but the proper ending comes before that, when Gawain is sulking over being saddled with a wife so old, ugly, and poor. And the loathly lady says, *Hey, listen up. Don't you know that age brings wisdom and discretion? That my ugliness means you'll never have to fear a rival? And, as for my low degree, don't forget that true gentility is no accident of birth but a quality of character.* The question I want to raise today is: *Why not just end the story there? Why the fairy tale? What does our desire for the second ending say about who we are?*"

On the faces of her students, Stella recognizes the customary mix of bafflement and boredom, sprinkled with the occasional soul-saving spark of real interest, of burgeoning thought. She folds her arms and leans back against her desk at the front of the room, awaiting a response. She can afford to be patient. She has all the time in the world.

Stella's own story has two endings as well. The proper ending goes like this: there was no baby. There was no pregnancy. As far as she knows, Stephen is still alive somewhere. Maybe he lives in a Zen monastery in Oregon, or maybe he sells Birkenstocks in a mall in Brandon. She never met his mother; he never met her kids. They never saw each other again.

The job and the house and the children's book really happened, though, and Percy too. Except that Percy teaches at Dalhousie, in Halifax, so they only see each other four or five times a year. Stella has learned to respect the role that geography plays in their mutual happiness. She suspects that happy-ever-after is simply beyond her, in practical terms. She's insufficiently abject, too schooled in the deconstruction of romance. Dispossessed, somehow, of the capacity for leaps of faith.

Jake, on the other hand, and much to Stella's surprise, made the leap; he remarried last year. Stella loves to tell people that Jake's new wife is a grandmother, which is true. But the fact is that Maggie's only two years older than Stella, and annoyingly possessed of the vitality (and body) of a thirty-five-year-old. Even more annoying is the fact that she's almost impossible to hate: a clear-eyed, straight-talking schoolteacher who took an early-retirement package and bought herself a beach bar in Belize. She and Jake seem happy together; Stella pictures them standing side by side at the bar, spinning pastel froth in a blender and wiping counter tops, as the smell of jasmine floats on the night breeze.

Charlotte has gone on to great things — she wins fellowships, she publishes, she gives papers. Stella figures that, for Charlotte, just getting up in the morning and walking through the world in her own treacherous skin is torment enough. Or maybe not.

Once in a while, Stella decides, if only for a moment, that she can stand the idea of Jake being happy. Or even Charlotte.

Other times, though, she wonders whether happiness is even

the point. She was happy with Stephen, for a while. But beyond the hill of wonders lies the whole world.

And she has to ask herself "Would Stephen have tasted as sweet without the savour of Nigel's heartache?" Probably not.

And she wonders "What *was* Stephen, anyway? Angel, daemon, emanation, maybe a *koan*, a Zen question that can't be answered. Revelation, redemption, homecoming. Erotic megavitamin? Maybe just a horny kid."

No matter. A story like theirs is a gift which must be received with unquestioning gratitude and put to the best possible use.

# EPILOGUE

## June 2000

FRIDAY

The directions on the discharge sheet say "Remove the dressings three days after the surgery." So this morning, I steeled myself to the task of peeling surgical adhesive from my butt cheeks and beheld a perineum that called to mind the phrase "black arsehole of Calcutta."

Before he left for school this morning, Zak reminded me about his quarter-final ball game on Sunday. He really wants me to go, but I'm not sure if I can manage to sit on a bleacher all afternoon without my inflatable donut, which I'm too proud to use in public. Besides, the games are psychically painful enough anyway. All season, Zak has not hit the ball once. He has struck out. He has gotten his walks on ball four. He has gotten his walks after being hit by a wild pitch. On these occasions, he limps manfully to first base, and my heart just squeezes, his adolescent lope and held-back tears more than I can bear. I promised, "Do my best. I'm going for a massage after work, so don't forget your key, okay?"

A few years ago, when I was still at the university, I was having what I called "a butt crisis," and had to bring an ice pack to work, which I stashed in the department fridge and slipped underneath me during office hours. One day, I was going over a paper with a student, a rather prim young man named Ben, I believe. Anyhow, we got into a bit of a discussion on some point, and I forgot about my butt crisis and got up to pull a book from the shelf. As I turned back, I saw Ben's glance resting on the seat of my chair, where a bright blue icepack in the shape of a teddybear sweated and melted under the heat of my inflamed innards. It was one of those existential moments, the kind that leaves you asking yourself, *How did I get here?*

A similar moment occurred tonight; I hauled my blackened backside out of a sitz-bath, and, as I tenderly towelled off, was dismayed to see that Band-Aid shadows — the sticky adhesive residue of my recently removed surgical dressing — were still plainly visible on both cheeks. Larry had quietly massaged his way around them this afternoon, without saying a word. For some reason, getting back into the tub once again, to scrub off the evidence, I remembered a day more than twenty years ago, on the Island. The summer I worked at the Forestry nursery, the summer I met Charlie, I guess. And Jake. Anyway, there'd been a hot spell, and a group of us from camp loaded into a pickup and drove to a place called The Potholes. It was a small river, which because of some geological accident, formed deep swimming holes in the rock. The first pool, nearest the road, was for families. There were blankets and picnic baskets and radios, kids splashing in the water, babies in drooping diapers toddling on the grass. We walked on to a second pool a short way up the trail through the woods, stripped off our clothes, cracked a case of Pil, and played in the water. After an hour or so, my co-workers were all dozing on the bank or complaining about the camp cook, so I said to Delia, Let's see what's above the falls. We got back in the water and swam across the pool to a rocky ledge, where minuscule rainbows glittered in the cascade of water from the hill above. We slid and giggled trying to get a purchase on those smooth slippery rocks, but eventually we both got over the ledge, and found ourselves in a stream no more than a foot deep. We could see another falls about fifty yards ahead, so we pulled ourselves upstream, sliding over cool rocks hazed and slick with electric green moss, laughing at the tickle of old stone on breast or belly, the sun hot on our shoulders, the rest of our bodies submerged in icy green. We slithered like primeval creatures, seeking purchase with fingers and toes, making our way to the source. The uppermost ledge was sharp, and we lingered under the falls a moment, letting the icy water fill our mouths, then heaved ourselves over the ledge, and slid down into another pool of the most innocent green. The banks here were not grass but rock, darker than the pool below but smooth, ancient, welcoming. Around the edges of the pool were other creatures, young men, two of them. And a third sitting yoga fashion on a ledge above the falls, strumming a mandolin. All of us naked. "Good afternoon, ladies," said the blond one, his long legs dangling in the water. The reddish-gold hair that swirled on the skin of his thighs looked like a rune of the deepest meaning. The dark-haired one on the other edge smiled, and passed Delia a jug of Gallo Chablis. "Welcome," he said. The mandolin player strummed, joints were passed, laughter and lazy talk, warm sun and cool green water. Time stopped, we were beings at home in a green world, with no duty but pleasure.

I thought about that day as I gingerly scrubbed my backside. I wondered how this could have happened, how the word *haemorrhoidectomy* could ever have become part of my vocabulary, not to mention part of my experience. Any time I remember that day at The Potholes, I think, who could blame me, who could blame anyone who'd lived a day like that day at The Potholes, for thinking that we were exempt? Who could blame us for thinking that we could glide against the stream undamaged, that our freedoms were limitless and our entitlement absolute?

⌒

SATURDAY

The best way to fully understand the dimensions of ancient Greek tragedy, as described by Aristotle, is to attempt to take a shit with ten stitches in your arsehole. *Anagnorisis* — the bitter discovery that the bathroom cannot be avoided indefinitely. *Peripeteia,* my heaving guts initiating the sudden reversal in fortune from analgesic happiness to bodily disaster. Wanting no *chorus* to comment on unfolding events, I send the children downstairs with licence to watch TV till they bleed from the eyeballs. And I close the door, firmly, on the dog.

*Hamartia* — the fatal error in judgement was popping two Tylenol 3 about ten minutes too late. *Hubris* to think I could ignore not divine warnings but the urgency of the body. *Pathos* — violent physical pain, accompanied by heaving, screams, moans, cries, prayers, tears. The label of the mouthwash bottle swims before my bleared eyes — I believe the Oracle's message is: *For best results use full strength.*

And finally, *catharsis* — purgation, purification. Afterward, I float down the corridor, to take, cheerfully, to my bed, feeling that I have fully participated in an action that is serious and of great magnitude.

Within an hour of the event, I get three phone calls — Gretz, Diana, and Percy. Perhaps those who love me sensed some telepathic twang, and I am able to describe, in varying detail, the experience. Gretz sings a few bars of "Ring of Fire" and makes me laugh; she's due in a couple of weeks, twins. Amazing what they can do with *in vitro* these days. "Just you wait," I tell her, laughing. Diana is motherly, concerned, offers to take the kids off my hands, despite the fact that she and Bill and the boys are packing for a month-long camping trip up the Alaska Highway. Just to piss her off, I say, "You know, Di, I've discovered that Tylenol 3 achieves in ten minutes the state that results from a full hour of yoga." She is unfazed: "Yeah, but you don't need to refill your prescription for yoga, do you? And it doesn't constipate you, either."

I'm still mulling the sinister implications of that information when Percy calls from Halifax, and I guess what endears me the most is that he pretends not to be wondering whether I'll be sackworthy again when we meet at the conference next month. We are scrupulous about making demands on each other. I tend to think of Percy not as an answer, or even a statement, but rather as a series of interesting questions. I am blessed in my friends.

As I lie there in a codeine drift, after these calls, I think of Michelle for the first time in years — that lovely hopeful woman, adjusting her sunglasses as she steps from the seaplane. She would be in her mid-fifties now, still regally tall, her hair still shiny and dark. The years have been kind to her. I figure that shortly after the affair with Charlie ended, she went to work for a different company, and has for more than twenty years been the executive assistant to a corporate guy who treats her pretty decently, never more than the occasional squeeze on the shoulder, a man who describes her to his cronies as his "girl," as in "I'll get my girl to call yours." This is okay by Michelle. By the time she met her husband, an accountant with the company, it was too late for children. Michelle's doctor mentioned "adhesions," he mentioned "scar tissue," but Michelle felt no need to pursue the matter. So she and her husband have what they both describe as a "nice lifestyle." They travel, they redecorate their home, they take loving care of their two pure-bred dogs, standard poodles is my guess. They're saving up for a retirement condo in Palm Desert.

For about a decade, Michelle hated me. She remembered every detail: the sun glinting off the water of the harbour, my dusty jeans, the pills on my Cowichan sweater, the curl of unkempt hair teasingly bouncing in the seabreeze. The utter carelessness with which I walked away. She thinks I never gave her a second thought.

After a decade or so, though, and without even really noticing it, Michelle forgot about me and actively hated Charlie. Maybe it was the times, maybe a book she read or a movie she saw, but, suddenly, the thought of the sharp crease in his grey-flannel pants, or even just the sight of two glasses side by side on a table by a sunny window, and something would just seize in her — she'd find herself choked with hatred, which evolved over the years into mere irritation.

But these days, Michelle rarely thinks of either of us. She can't even remember my name. She doesn't know I gave up pleading innocent a long time ago.

11:30. The dog groans out of her basket, wanders over to her water dish, laps messily, sighs. Then *kaa-tipp, kaa-tipp*, down the hall. Going straight to her side of the bed, *ka-tip-pa, ka-tip-paah*. A lengthy pause, another sigh, clump, scrape, jangle, the scrabble of claws on hardwood. She smacks her black and pink lips six or seven times, farts gently, and sleeps. She won't be with us much longer.

No random beeps, not for a few months. The battery finally wound itself down, I guess.

SUNDAY

Just as we're searching for the ball glove, Jake calls to check on Zak's travel plans for next week. Maggie's daughter and little grandson are flying down too. "I can't wait to see them all," Jake says, uncharacteristically gushy. "It's as if I couldn't know what it is to love a child till I became a grandparent."

*Fuck you, asshole*, I think, but do not say. I *do* say, "Step-grandparent, you mean. So it's true. Tropical climes do soften the brain."

"Fuck you, Stella," he says cheerfully, and not without affection.

The guy had his uses, I can't deny it. For one thing, he was angry enough for three or four people. He committed the outrages I could no longer risk. I remember how, in undergrad, we stored our belongings in cardboard boxes, or in plastic milk crates emblazoned with the words *Property of Freshtest Dairies*. A year or two into grad school, we bought Sterilite baskets at Kmart, and garage-sale dressers with layers of paint that told their history like the rings on an ancient tree. It *mattered*, but we never got around to acknowledging that it did. So by the time I went out to Eaton's and hauled a bunch of cartons into the house, Jake just gave me a dark look and (ineptly) assembled the particleboard closet organizers I'd bought. We were both thinking, I know we were, that a closet consultant comes next, a crisply dressed woman with a leather-bound sketch pad and a Cross pen, scribbling a cheerful estimate on a Storage System Uniquely Suited to Our Individual Needs.... He got out before it came to that.

The semifinals, a breezy June day. The Eagles are down 7 to 5 in the bottom of the eighth. Zak has walked once and struck out once. Miranda is two bleachers below, giggling with her buddies, and a woman I know only as "Cody's mom" has handed me her child to hold while she goes for some Cokes. I'm too embarrassed to explain why the weight of a two-year-old is problematic, so I settle him gingerly on my lap, and inhale the clean smell of his fine black hair lifted up to me by the breeze. Beyond the ball field is a green expanse, a soccer field, I guess, but no game in progress. A few runners, a young couple lolling in the shade of a tree, and on a slight knoll at the edge of the field, a young man, dark-haired, dressed all in black, moving with the slow wisdom of centuries, serious and focused, his feet firm and definite on the earth, his head still as his body rises and falls in an ancient dance of moving meditation. I sense Cody's mom approaching, sitting down, faintly hear her voice saying, 'Great, just in time, Zak's at bat,' but I am concentrating, straining my middle-aged eyes at the figure on the knoll in the distance as I hand the child back to his mother, and accept the red and white cup from her outstretched hands — then CRACK. Cheers, Zak running, the outfield scrambling, but the ball bounces deep into right field, a three-run RBI. The game's not over, but Zak's team has a chance now. If the other team doesn't score in the next inning, the Eagles are in the finals. My son smiles up at the stands, his face alight. Miranda squeals with excitement, "Aw right, bro!" Joy stirs inside my chest and opens like a flower. I watch with amazed pleasure as each of Zak's teammates gives him the high five, as the coach thuds a backslap between his narrow shoulders. I'm thinking that this calls for a celebration, a burger and fries after the game, maybe.

I'm thinking about varieties of available bliss — like the sharp tang of vinegar hitting hot French fries. Like the way Delbert McClinton smiles and moves his hips when he sings the words "You, babe." Like finding a piece of blue glass in the surf, or hearing the spine-tingling blend of voices in the finale of *The Marriage of Figaro* ... or this day.

The next batter has struck out by the time I remember to look again for the young man dressed in black, and of course he's gone by then — vanished without a trace — and the lovers and runners are gone too. The field is empty but for a few crows — stiff-legged and clumsy — patiently mining the midsummer grass.

*Only the bird understands the textbook of the rose:*
  *For not every reader knows the inner meaning of the page.*
*O you who would learn the section on love from the book of*
    *knowledge —*
  *I fear that you do not know how to fathom it by research.*

Hafiz, *The Book of Sufi*

## REFERENCES

Bulfinch, Thomas. *Bulfinch's Mythology*, Abr. Dell, 1959.

—. Bulfinch's Mythology: *The Age of Chivalry and Legends of Charlemagne*. Doubleday, n.d.

Hamilton, Edith. *Mythology: Timeless Tales of Gods and Heroes*. New American Library, 1940. Repr. 1969.

Hope-Moncrieff, A.R. *The Romance of Chivalry*. Newcastle, 1976.

Shah, Idries. *The Way of the Sufi*. Penguin, 1968.